PRAISE FOR THE WEB PAIGE CHRONICLES

"Web Paige Chronicles offers a refreshing and empowering role model for young adults. By eschewing this iGeneration's stereotypical malaise in favor of positive curiosity with technology, Iasiello folds practical cybersecurity guidance into a relatable story." -Scott Schober, author of Hacked Again

Emilio Iasiello is a cyber-security expert who has written a novel that is not only a modern and realistic coming-of-age book that either boys or girls will enjoy, it helps them learn to deal with such modern problems as cyber bullying, hacking, sexting, online predators and more. Though the main characters are junior high aged, older readers will enjoy this quick read, and learn a great deal about safely negotiating modern technology and social interactions. Highly recommended for schools and parents to share with their tweens and teens— though there's plenty for adults to learn about internet safety in here too. He has added a fine reference section at the end of this novel for more useful cyber-safety tips.

The Web Paige Chronicles
by Emilio Iasiello
©2018, Emilio Iasiello

Tell-Tale Publishing Group, LLC
Swartz Creek, MI 48473

THISTLE

Printed in the United States of America

For Betta and Mimmuccio who will be infinitely smarter than their dad.

The Web Paige Chronicles

Emilio Iasiello

Chapter One

The day I was born, I yelled so loudly after the doctor smacked my bum that my mother knew I was cut from the same bolt of cloth as the women of her family. Barely two minutes old, I was outspoken and opinionated and let everyone in the room know how I felt about that bum-smack, especially the doctor.

I come from what my mom calls solid Godfrey stock. All the women are strong-willed and ready at a moment's notice to offer their opinions on everything ranging from local politics to the type of brown sugar to use in a proper apple cobbler, whether you asked them or not. Even now, Grandma Betty (the name I call Beatrice Dolores) has no problem letting you know the Washington Nationals baseball team will never win a championship as long as they keep treating their players like spoiled children instead of grown men. She has what my mom refers to as an acid tongue.

I'm named after three generations of these Godfreys women, grandmothers, all on my mother Letitia's side: - my great-great-grandmother Wilhelmina Lucynell Godfrey; my great-grandmother Eugenia Gladys Godfrey; and finally, my grandmother Beatrice Dolores Godfrey

While I love my name, Wilhelmina Eugenia Beatrice Paige is a mouthful for anyone, including my parents. To them I'm just Willy, even at twelve years old, unless I'm being scolded for something like forgetting my chores or interrupting grown-up talk. Then both my mother and father will address me by my full name in stern voices. That's when I know I'm in real trouble. Fortunately, that doesn't happen all that often. I'm a pretty good kid for the most part, but sometimes my curiosity gets the better of me, leading me down what my dad refers to as unpleasant rabbit holes.

While family prefers calling me Willy or Wilhelmina, everyone else just calls me Web.

I didn't like the nickname at first, truth be told. Web reminds me of webs which instantly reminds me of spiders, and spiders remind me of, well, spiders – ugly, creepy crawly things that scare me half to death. Nothing's worse than running into a spider web either. You jump around like you're practicing karate trying to get the unseen silk strands off your skin. Yuck. It gives me the shivers just thinking about it.

So, you must be wondering how I got that nickname, especially since you know my feelings on webs. It's simple. Pretty much the way most people get nicknames – through their friends.

The Web Paige Chronicles

My bestie Tamara called me Web after I helped her install an operating system update on her home computer. An operating system is what makes a computer's functions run. It sounds complicated but it's not so hard if you know what you're doing.

OK. I know what you're thinking. Web is a computer geek.

And to answer that charge I proudly say, "yes, I am." I'm naturally curious about things, as you now know, and there is nothing more fascinating than computers – not just the amazing cool things that they do, or the things we can do on them like edit movies or play games, but how they work. Such little pieces of gadgetry allow us to do pretty much everything. Our cell phones now have more computer power than the computers that helped NASA send people to the moon. True story.

But getting back to the nickname. I was over at Tamara's house listening to music when she said, "The store gave me a bum disk. I loaded it and did everything the directions said. When it didn't work, I loaded it again. Now I think it broke my computer. I can't even get the operating system to work." After beating around the bush, she let out a groan in frustration. "I need help," she finally admitted.

I didn't have the heart to tell her she was doing something wrong. "Let me have a look," I said and started to fidget around with the device. When I saw what the problem was, I did a hard restart. Problem solved.

"You sure are a whiz with computers. I'm going to call you Webopedia from now on. You're like a walking encyclopedia about computers and stuff."

If I'm being honest, Webopedia didn't stick immediately. When word got around at school about fixing her computer, my friends started calling me different variations. Betta DiMeo called me Webmaster, and Andrea Tomas preferred to call me Webpage. But as time went on, everyone settled on the shortened amalgamation of these nicknames – Web.

And you know what? I think it suits me best.

See, Web has a double meaning. Yes, it's a cute moniker that references my favorite hobby in the world – computers. But it's also the composition of the first letters of each of my grandmother's names: Wilhelmina Eugenia Beatrice.

And so Web Paige was born.

I'm in my room trying to read one of my dad's computer security manuals when I hear the phone ring. I don't hear my name being called by my mom until the third time.

"Wilhelmina! Phone!"

I jump to my feet and race to the phone in the upstairs hallway. When I answer it, I hear Tamara's panicked voice on the other end.

"Web! Thank God, you're home! I don't know who else to reach out to."

"What's wrong?"

"My mom needs your help!" Even though the cell phone connection isn't all that great, I can tell she's on the border of crying.

"Slow down, T," I tell her, using my nickname for her. "Tell me what happened."

"Web, I don't know. My mom was sending emails for my birthday party and suddenly the people she emailed are calling her and telling her to stop sending them spam. You know her – the only spam my mother knows is the one that's canned."

I smile when I hear that. T's mom is like many grownups when it comes to technology. Now, I'm good with computers. Even though I'm only twelve, I can do more with computers than most adults, which is weird when you consider how much older they are. But it's like my father says – just because people are older doesn't make them smarter and that's especially true when it comes to computers. Some grown-ups don't want to try to understand how computers work, and that's what usually gets them in trouble. They don't know how to fix the simplest things, or they click on things that they shouldn't. They just want to know the time, they don't want to know how the clock is made, as the saying goes.

"Can you help?" she asks.

"I'll do what I can," I say. "Let me ask you some questions first."

I ask her a bunch of questions about when did her mom noticed that things were wrong, what exactly did the spam emails say, when did she first hear that the people in her contact list had received the email. I write down everything like my father tells me to do. Preparation. Preparation. Preparation. The more information at hand, the better you'll be able to figure out what's wrong and how to fix it.

"All right. I'm going to have to see the emails. Tell your mom to leave everything as it is and most importantly, don't delete anything. I'll be right over."

"Thanks Web!"

I hang up the phone and go over to my bookshelf. I scan the titles: How to Troubleshoot Your Problems, Maintaining Your PC, Data Recovery Techniques. Many kids my age like to read adventure and fantasy books, stories about vampires and wizards and love and stuff like that. Me, I like to know how computers work, and when I can, how to keep them running. My father tells me I have an inquisitive brain, which is a rare thing, he says, especially in today's world of information overload. He says it will keep me occupied for a while.

I finally find what I'm looking for on the floor of my room under my bookbag – The PC Help Desk – Common Fixes and Solutions.

"Ha!" I say. "There you are."

I stuff it into my bookbag and sling the bag over my shoulders. I check myself in the mirror. With my glasses and mouth retainer, I look like a professional Geek Squad member.

"Okay, Web," I say to the reflection in front of me. "Time to score some karma points."

"You want a tuna fish sandwich?" my mother asks when she sees me bound down the steps. She's in her nurse's uniform and making one for her shift break this evening at the hospital. She's working nights this month, which means I only see her in the afternoons. She always tries to make what I like when she works nights to make up for having to experience my father's cooking. Dad's best work in the kitchen comes in the form of pancakes and eggs. He's not so good with understanding the delicate equation of heat and time when it comes to cooking inside an oven.

"Maybe later. I'm on a flash job." Flash jobs are what my dad calls jobs that needed to have been done the day before instead of right now.

"Oh, a flash job," my mother says, bagging her sandwich along with a bag of chips and an apple. "Who messed up their computer now?"

For the past month, I've been helping friends and family with their computers, laptops, and even iPhones. Usually, people went to my father for matters like these, but he has been so busy and working all the time my mother told me I should step up and assume that responsibility. She says it gives me karma points when I help others. Since she's a nurse, I'm sure she has thousands of karma points stacked up someplace.

"Tamara's mother has an issue. I think her email account got hacked but I'm not sure. I have to go check it out."

"I swear, that woman gets into more hot water than a hardboiled egg."

My mother looks at the clock on the wall. It's almost three in the afternoon.

"I want you back before your father comes home. He's making roasted chicken."

I give my mom a look. My dad doesn't do well with chicken.

"I know, I know," she says before I even get a word out. "He wants to try, we should let him. But that doesn't mean I don't have a backup plan."

She opens the refrigerator and shows me a covered tin.

"Baked ziti," she says. "Put it in the oven and heat at 350 for fifteen minutes. Break in case of emergency."

I give her a big smile. Mom always thinks ahead.

"Sure thing, Mom."

I'm almost out the door, when I hear, "Excuse me young lady aren't you forgetting something?"

I poke my head around the door. My mother touches her cheek with her finger.

"My bad!"

I smile awkwardly and run to her and give her a big kiss.

"Back before five, understand? And be careful."

"Mom," I say to her, rolling my eyes. She's always worrying about something. She tells me her revenge is going to be when I have kids. I shrug it off each time she says it.

Outside, I retrieve my bike from the garage. It's pink with colored ribbons on the handlebars. It's pretty beat up because I do a lot of bike riding. That's the only way kids can go anyplace in Falls

River. Some places and some houses are just too far to walk.

My mother doesn't mind me riding to Tamara's house because it's only the next street over. For the most part, our neighborhood is safe. Three of the families living in the community have a parent that's a police officer. My father says that seeing police cars parked in driveways is a pretty good criminal deterrent.

He must be right, I think to myself as I put on my helmet. The neighborhood hasn't recorded a single crime in three years.

Tamara waits for me on her front porch as I bike toward her house. She's biting her thumb nail like she does when she's waiting for the teacher to put a test on her desk at school.

"Finally!" says my best friend. "What kept you?" We've known each other since forever, which is why I know she's not really cross with me, just anxious. My mom says when we first moved to town, we didn't know a soul. That first Saturday, we went to the park and she set me in the sandpit. A little bit later, T's mom showed up and did the same. They even have a picture of it – T and I in our diapers, playing with buckets and shovels. Besties ever since.

I roll my eyes as I set my bike down on the front lawn. Tamara is also a future actress. She always wins the lead parts in all our school plays, and if I'm being honest, she's a bit of a drama queen. Even now I can't really tell if she's that worried or just exaggerating. She'll probably walk the red carpet and win an Oscar one day.

I run up to the top step. T is taller than me so we're on the same level. Right now, her normally soft brown eyes are wide with excitement.

"Our computer is wrecked," she laments, her tight corn row braids swinging as she gestures wildly. "My party is ruined!"

"I'm here now, T," I say. "Take me to the PC."

Tamara's house is two stories with a wide front porch with a swing and two large chairs. The interior is a melding of eclectic tastes; art on the walls range from African-themed art and masks to Picasso reprints. T's mom is an art teacher at the local high school and her father is a curator of the Smithsonian Museum of African Art in D.C.

T leads me into the kitchen where her mother, Mrs. Okafur, sits with a cup of tea, nervously tapping her fingers on the table. She lets out a sigh when she hears us enter.

"Willy, thank goodness you're here," she says. "I don't know what happened. I sent out the e-vites two days ago, and then today I log into my account and find this."

She shows me the laptop. On screen is her inbox for her webmail account. There are five new messages with subject lines that say: "Why did you send me that?" "Spam Alert!" and "Something's wrong with your email."

"I don't send spam," she says, "whatever that is. The only spam I know…"

"No problem, Mrs. O," I say as I scan through the inbox. Six other messages that she has already read reflect the same tone of the unread emails. "Is this all of them?"

"So far," she says, taking a sip of tea. "I sent out twenty-two invites. The rest haven't responded yet."

I pull up a chair and take control of the keyboard.

"OK," I say. "Let's take a look."

"Please do. Anything you can do to help is greatly appreciated, Willy," Mrs. Okafur says.

I check the "sent" folder of the email account to see the messages she sent to her friends. They were all sent on the same today and in succession.

"This is the first time something like this has happened?" I ask her.

"Yes."

I nod. I scan her inbox as well as her junk mail and deleted mails to see if I can find any suspicious email that might have been sent to her and that she had accidentally thought was from a legitimate person.

"How's your mom doing?" Mrs. Okafur asks me. "I didn't see her the other night at the church diaper drive."

"She's fine," I respond. "She's working nights."

"God bless that woman," Mrs. O says. "The hours she puts into the hospital, they should name a wing after her."

After I complete my initial investigation I turn to T's mom.

"Can I ask you a question?"

"Of course, you can," Mrs. O says.

"Do you have a strong password protecting your account?"

"I don't know. I think so. It's Tamara's birthday."

"Ah," I say, immediately understanding the situation. One of the most common security mistakes that people make involves passwords. They are usually too simple, or else they reuse the same passwords for every account they have. This is bad because if one of these accounts gets compromised and the bad guys know the password, they will try it against every account they think the victim has. The same password means access into all those accounts.

"What is it? What's the matter?" T blurts out.

"The password is too simple. It's all numbers, am I right?"

"How do you know that?"

"Human nature," I say. I try to sound authoritative like my father when he reaches conclusions. "People generally approach passwords using the KISS approach."

"The KISS what?"

"Keep It Simple Stupid," I say.

"With everything requiring a password now-a-days, what are people expected to do? Emails, social media, insurance, healthcare... everything is done online, and everyone requires a password. How are people supposed to memorize all of them?"

"Human nature is to simplify – not complicate – their lives. I tell her. "And that's what the bad guys are counting on."

Mrs. O frowns and takes another sip of tea.

How can someone guess numbers?" she asks after some thought.

"That's the beauty of it. They don't have to. The bad guys use a special software program that launches a 'dictionary attack'. That's a process that systematically runs every word in a dictionary as a potential password. It does it with numbers too. It starts with one character and goes up to how many characters are required to break the password."

"I don't see anything beautiful about it," Mrs. O says with an annoyed tone, sitting up rigidly in her seat. "That's frightening."

"I don't mean it that way," I say trying to assuage the situation. "It's just that considering that everyone needs a password, some smart people create these tools to help them break them. The human mind is amazing in how it works."

"They should use it for good."

"They do. Organizations can use the very same tool to ensure that their employees have strong passwords before a bad guy breaks in."

"Oh, dear," Mrs. O says. "Can you help me make a new one?"

"No problem, Mrs. O. Consider passwords to be the first line of defense. Like a fence. You should make them as strong as possible but understand that they alone won't keep all bad guys out."

Mrs. Okafur nods her head. I think she's getting it.

"The best passwords," I continue, "should be at least eight characters long. They should include a mixture of upper and lower-case letters, numbers, and special characters."

"Wait a second," Mrs. Okafur says. "What do you mean by special characters?"

"You know. Things like '@,' '#,' '&', or '*', for example."

"I didn't know you could use those. But that seems like an awful lot of things to remember," Mrs. Okafur says. "How can I remember that?"

"It's not as hard as it looks. Think of a phrase you are apt to remember like, 'walk the dog' but substitute the special characters and numbers for some of the letters. So instead of just being 'walkthedog,', your password would be 'W@lkth3d*g.'"

Mrs. Okafurs's face brightens.

"What did I tell you, Mom," T says. "Web's a genius. Since we have to walk our dog Chester every day that should be pretty easy for me to remember."

"That helps," Mr. Okafur says. "But be honest with me, Willy. Will this guarantee that my password won't be broken, or stolen, or whatever it is that they did with this one?"

"Not exactly," I say. "But it makes it more difficult to break. Bad guys are usually looking for easy marks. If they find that it's taking too long to break your password, they'll usually stop and look for someone else to try and exploit. For them, it's a numbers game."

Mrs. Okafur shakes her head.

"That's too bad that there are people out there looking to take advantage of the rest of us online," she says. "When I was your age, we worried about people stealing our mail. Now, they don't even have to leave their homes to steal things."

"That's right," I say. "But like my father says, cyber security is everyone's responsibility. If we are going to use this technology, we have to know how to use it responsibly and that includes breaking bad security habits like using weak passwords. In this case, they used your account to send out spam. That's better than using your email to access other areas of yours."

Mrs. Okafur finally smiles.

"You're right. Thanks for your help as always, Willy," she says. "I'm going to change all my passwords immediately. You know, that would be a good part time job for you. Cyber trouble shooter. You're a walking – what do they call them? Help desks?"

"Cyber trouble shooter," I muse. "I like it."

"Well, now that problem is solved, can we make sure people are coming to my party?" T says.

"Of course, dear."

"You know, T. While I'm here, we should discuss how we are going to approach our science project."

"I meant to ask you two – what are you girls doing?"

"We're trying to figure out how different search engines work," I say, matter-of-factly. "Each engine has an algorithm that helps find what you're looking for."

"Since these companies don't like to share their proprietary formula," Tamara says. "We're identifying search terms and running them in five different search engines and comparing what they find and in what order."

"I should have guessed," Mrs. Okafur says, laughing to herself as she types away on her laptop. "You know, when I was your age we were making volcanoes erupt with baking soda."

"Very retro, Mrs. O."

Later, T walks me outside to my bicycle. It's a little past four o'clock. It's still warm for early September. The sky is just beginning to darken at its far edges. I stand up my bicycle and prepare to hop on it.

"Thanks for the help, Web."

"No problem. Anytime I can help, you know the number."

"My mom's right. You should be like one of those geek squad people. I bet there are lots of people who don't know about what to do with passwords."

"That was the easy part. There are lots of things people can do when it comes to passwords. The problem is, it takes some effort and most people don't like to do extra effort."

"Like what other kinds of things?" Tamara asks.

"Let's see. For one, frequently changing all your passwords is a good way of staying one step ahead of the bad guys. Even if they have an old password of yours, by frequently changing them, they won't be able to use it."

"Yeah, that makes sense."

"Never share your passwords with anyone, either. You'd be surprised how loose-lipped people are."

"True that," Tamara laughs. "Betta DiMeo can't keep a secret if her life depended on it."

"Keep strong passwords and keep them to yourself."

"I heard that. See you tomorrow, Web."

"See ya, T."

It's a short ride home but I can't help thinking about what Mrs. O said. I am a regular walking, talking help desk. I can replace memory chips, troubleshoot error messages, install just about any software that's out there, and answer most questions people have when it comes to computers. Chances are that if someone has a problem I can pretty much solve it.

I owe a lot of this to my father, Cornelius. He's a computer forensics expert. That's a fancy title for a person that knows way more about computers than pretty much the rest of the population. He works for the police in Washington, D.C., which means he helps the good guys put away the bad guys.

And there's a lot of bad guys in cyberspace.

When grownups ask me what my father does, I try to explain that his job is to find, recover, and preserve digital evidence. Once I see their blank expressions, I tell them that computer forensics examiners are like regular forensics examiners that they see on TV shows like "CSI." Both use science to investigate criminal acts. The only difference is that the clues my father looks for are digitally-based, meaning that they consist of programming code, metadata, emails, and generally any computer-related technology.

The Web Paige Chronicles

I learn a lot from my father who sometimes walks me through the cases that he has worked. Whether it be a new scam, cyber criminal thefts, or cyber spies' exploits against government organizations, he breaks down how the operations occurred, and why they were or were not successful. He teaches me how to approach the practical and technical applications of computers with a thoughtful and critical eye. He shows me the proper ways to collect data, and the thorough way analysis must be conducted to get at the truth.

"The truth is always there if you look hard enough," my father always tells me. "It may not be easy to find, and sometimes it's not meant to be. But if you work hard enough, you'll find it."

My mother is not a computer expert. As she puts it, "When it comes to that bizzy-bappy stuff, I'm all thumbs."

Where my father is a virtual helper, my mom helps people in the real world. She manages a group of emergency room nurses at the Fall Rivers hospital. She says she likes to help those who need it immediately and the emergency room is the best place to have an immediate impact on a person's health. She has seen it all – gunshots, stabbings, people hurt in car accidents and falls. A nurse is the point person in patient care. They are typically the first healthcare professional someone sees and the one that frequently checks in on patients. My mom says a nurse has to do a bunch of jobs and roles but needs to have two things to really make a difference in a person's life: compassion and empathy. Compassion motivates strangers to help each other and empathy allows you to put yourself in another person's position and understand what troubles or suffering they are experiencing.

"A little kindness goes a long way, Willy," she reminds me during times when I'm mad at a friend or boy at school. "You may not know why a person says or does something mean. Putting yourself in their shoes gives you a different perspective. It doesn't justify what they've done, but it helps you understand why they did it."

She was always saying smart things like that.

We live in Fall Rivers, Virginia. It's a small town right across the Potomac River from Washington, D.C. Grownups always say it's a good place for us kids. There's enough elbow room (their words) and has everything a town should have: schools, banks, two gas stations, a library, coffee shops, three different churches, and a Safeway and a Giant supermarket.

Parks are plentiful and safe, so that's fun for us, and we look forward to the two town festivals – one in the summer and one in the fall. When Halloween rolls around, houses look fun, and the holidays are always full of bright, colorful, winking lights.

When I get to my house, I've come to a decision. I will provide computer help services to those who need it. And trust me, if you knew the people I know, you'd understand that it's a self-perpetuating business model. So many people don't understand how to keep their information, and more importantly, themselves safe when using computers or surfing the Internet.

My neighbors and friends deserve to be safe in cyberspace as well as in our hometown.

And I'm just the kid that can help then stay that way.

Chapter Two

Unfortunately, I arrive too late to rescue our dinner from setting off the smoke alarm. I enter the kitchen to see my father juggling a smoldering baking pan with oversized oven mitts while trying to close the oven door with his knee.

"Open a window," my father says as he places the pan on top of the stove. I can see the remains of the chicken, it's blackened legs sticking up. Poor bird never had a chance against my father's cooking.

I walk over to the sink and open the windows. Then I go into the living room and do the same, fanning the air furiously with a dishtowel until the incessant beeping of the alarm subsides.

"Do I dare ask?" I say.

"I think I left it in too long," he says to me, sheepishly.

"Noooooo," I say in my best condescending voice. It isn't often I get to tease my father. He looks at me and cocks an eyebrow. I smile and retrieve a garbage bag from the pantry closet.

"Do we have to?" he asks me, knowing what we do.

"It's for the best," I say. "We have to respect the dead."

"You are so hysterical my sides are going to split from laughing so hard."

"How is it," I continue after inspecting the oven, "that you can break down computer code but find it hard to distinguish broil from bake?"

"Everyone's brain works differently," he says, chuckling loudly. For a certified computer geek, my father never takes himself too seriously and has a pretty good sense of humor. Oh, and when I say certified, that's not just an expression. He has more than twenty IT-related certificates, so yeah, he's pretty much a geek.

He dumps the bird into the garbage.

"Well, how about pizza? My treat."

"Mom thought this would happen," I tell him. I go over to the refrigerator and remove the baked ziti.

"What's that?"

"Plan B."

"Your mom is a smart woman," he says, inspecting the contents of the tin. "I do love her baked ziti."

In the middle of dinner, I relate the story about Mrs. Okafur and her hacked email account. He listens thoughtfully, waiting for me to tell all the details before he offers a word. He always says the most important thing to do when investigating is to make sure you have all the facts before starting. That way you don't head down any wrong paths from the get-go.

"That is the reality of our times, I'm afraid," he says, when I'm finished. He tears two pieces off a loaf of bread. He hands one to me.

"So, what do you think?"

"You testing me?"

"Maybe…"

"Well, based on what you told me, I'd have to guess – weak password?"

"Bingo," I say.

He smiles and shakes his head.

"That doesn't surprise me. It doesn't matter how many times we preach it. People always insist on taking the path of least resistance when it comes to security protocols and procedures. Passwords are just the tip of the iceberg."

"But why?" I ask. "It's not a secret anymore. Making more resilient passwords is the first step in help strengthening your security. Sure, it might be hard to remember, but -"

"But nothing. You nailed it right there. People will always prefer convenience over security. That's the challenge for us. Educating people to make better informed decisions about how they approach their personal security. Sometimes it works, sometimes it doesn't."

I chew on my ziti. My father has a way of getting straight to the heart of matters.

"Mrs. O thinks I should help people like her that don't know enough about computers or the Internet. She says there's lots of people like her out there that need a little guidance."

My father thinks on this a moment and nods in approval.

"She's right," he says. "Admitting you have a problem is a step in the right direction."

"Yeah, I guess."

"So, is this going to be something like a part time job?"

"Kinda, but I don't want to necessarily charge people for helping them. I want to help people because they need the help. And they asked for it. If I charged them money, I don't know. It wouldn't feel the same. I want it to be more about the act, not what I get because I did it."

"You like the idea of helping people who can't help themselves."

"Yeah, I do. I really do."

"That's 'cause you have a good heart. Like your mother."

"So, you think that's a good idea?"

"No. I think it's a great idea."

Dad, my computer geek hero despite his cooking failures, sounded so proud of me I felt even happier about my decision.

Before lights out, I sit up in bed with a notebook and pen, brainstorming ideas. If I'm going to help people, I need a catchy name. Or a title. Or something that stands out and grabs people's attentions.

Dad is right. People either don't take their security seriously, or else don't know how to improve their security on their own. This has got to change. Sure, there are those that aren't going to change no matter what. They are going to be the difficult ones to influence. But it's the others I need to focus on. The ones that just don't know what to do or where to go.

That's where I come in. Acting locally to improve things globally.

I list name titles:

Cyber Trouble Shooter

Digital Protector

Help Desk Paladin

Cyber Ninja

Super IT Specialist

I review the names and make a face like I sucked on a lemon.

They all sound too, well, blah.

Yawning, I turn off the light and snuggle under the covers.

Maybe something will come to me in a dream. That's where most of my best ideas come from.

I see my mother in the kitchen when I come down for breakfast. She puts a wrapped sandwich into my lunchbox and sets it next to my bookbag on the counter near the door.

"Good morning, sunshine," she says as she uses a spatula to push scrambled eggs and bacon onto a plate. She sets it at my seat at the kitchen table. "Your father tells me you were able to fix Mrs. Okafur's computer."

"It was no big deal." I pour myself a cup of orange juice and sit down and start to dig in.

"Mrs. Okafur appreciated it. She called to let me know you were very helpful. She also told me she said you should start your own practice. So," she says, pouring herself a cup of coffee. "Are you going to open your own business?"

"I don't know if I want to open a whole business. I just want to help people. Like you, but doing the types of things that dad does. Does that make sense?"

My mother smiles.

"More than you know. I think that's a wonderful idea. As Grandma Betty always says, we may not be able to help everyone, but we sure can help someone. But don't you want to be paid for your time? There's nothing wrong being compensated for the services you will be providing."

"I know, but not in that way. It just seems like if I was getting paid to do something like this, it would lose its meaning. It's not about money; it's about making a difference."

"Karma points."

My eyes get big.

"Yes! Exactly! Karma points."

My mom smiles.

"You're earning plenty. Now, you better get those eggs down," she says, "or you're going to miss your bus."

Word got around school that I helped Mrs. Okafur with a computer problem, and kids kept coming up to me at recess and in between classes and asked about what happened and what I did to fix the problem. Kids are always amazed when grown-ups ask us for help, and even more amazed when we are able to give it. Unsurprisingly, the story got bigger and more complicated from one kid to another. By the time the last boy came up to me, you would have thought I stopped a global-spreading virus.

At lunch, I sit with T, Betta, and Josie. Josie talks about a boy in class that she won't admit that she likes but always seems to talk about. Josie is absolutely boy crazy and it seems like she has a different boy she crushes on every other week.

"He always tries to pass me notes," Josie laments. "What is it about boys that they can't take a hint?"

"Um, maybe it's because you're always making moony faces at him when he's not looking," Betta teases.

"Shut up! I do not!"

"For someone who doesn't like a boy you sure are blushing a lot," Tamara joins in.

"Whatever, believe what you like. But I'd rather talk about Web being the new 'it' girl around school."

I almost spit out my juice.

"I helped one grown-up. It's not like I cured cancer or anything."

"You're always so modest, Web," Betta says. "Bask in the glory while it lasts."

"Look, I don't want fame or anything like that. I just want to help everyone. Grown-ups, kids, everyone. Computers can be tricky things."

"True dat," says Tamara. "So, what's the hook?"

"The what?"

"What's your name going to be? If you're going to be a super hero, you gotta have a cool name."

"Oh," I say. "Thing is, I don't know what to call myself."

"How about, Wonder Girl?" Betta offers.

I stick my tongue out at her. Betta is always looking to jibe someone.

"You're like trying to level the playing field," Josie says. "Equalizing things between the bad and the good. Digital Equalizer?"

"Too sci-fi for my tastes," I say. I turn to Tamara. "What about you, T? Got any bright ideas?"

Tamara is busy looking at something in a book. She doesn't say anything for some time. Then she lets out a shout.

"A-ha!" she proclaims triumphantly. "I've got it!"

"Are you going to keep it to yourself or share it?" Josie asks.

"Oracle."

"Oracle? Like what the Greeks had?" Betta asks.

"Kind of," I say, getting Tamara's gist. "Oracles were like these mystical mediums that people went to for advice to help them out."

"That's perfect!" Betta says. "Oracle for hire."

"Cyber-oracle," Tamara corrects her.

"Hmmm," I say. "That's got a nice ring to it."

"Looks like someone's going to score 800 on their SSATs," Betta says.

"You really like it?" Tamara asks.

"Yeah, T. I like it a lot."

In art class, Tamara helps me design a flyer to pass around. Tamara may not be a whiz at computers, but she has an eye for art and can make things pop to attract attention. After what seems like forever, she hands me a bright yellow piece of paper with a clever graphic of me leaning against a computer giving a "thumb up." Dark, bold letters announce proudly.

CYBER ORACLE

"Holy smokes, T," I say. "This is amazing."

"You have your talents, I have mine. You know how to upload Apps; I know how to use them. Check these out."

She hands me a series of business cards. They read:

Cyber Oracle
Have a question? See the Oracle!
Pay Depends on the Size of the Job
Web Paige, Principal

"I know you said you didn't want to get paid, so I wasn't sure what to put there."

"No, it's perfect. This is great, T. Thanks so much."

"Just paying it forward."

I stop. That's it. That's how I will get paid.

"You're a genius, T!"

"What did I do now?"

"Paying it forward. It's not so much that I don't want to be paid as much as I want the people that I help to pay me by helping someone else that needs it. Depending on the size of the job I do for them, it could be one favor or more."

"Yeah, but what if they can't? I mean, not everyone is as savvy as you are when it comes to computers."

I bite my lip as I chew through this obstacle. My eyes brighten.

"Doesn't have to be with computers but just with things, you know? Not everyone is good at the same things. I help out a carpenter, for instance. He can help out an accountant with some work. The accountant can help out a family."

"You know, it might just work."

"I hope so."

After school, I can't wait to start on my new project. My dad is already home when I arrive, and I tell him my plan and show him the flyers. He gives his approval and helps me as I go around the neighborhood. We insert my new flyers and business cards into people's mailboxes, underneath door knockers, and under the welcome mats of front steps. When the last flyer and card are fixed behind a screen door, dad and I drink a soda on the front steps in front of our house.

"You think I'll get any customers?" I ask him.

"Well, let's see. Last time I checked, there were around 300 million Internet users in the United States alone. That, and the fact that more than 80 percent of homes have at least one computer, yeah, I think you'll have a lot of work to do."

That reassuring sentiment is suddenly replaced by a horrible thought sweeping through my mind. A chill runs up and down my spine like a spider.

"What if I can't help them? What if I don't know how to fix a problem?"

Dad chuckles in his way that shakes his entire upper body shake.

"Trust in your skills, Willy. But look, I'm not going to lie to you. When it comes to technology, you're not going to be able to fix everything. Case and point. One case I worked on last month, we had seized a suspect's computer. The system was so old that it was running an operating system that the company didn't make security patches for anymore. There were so many viruses and adware on the system, I was surprised any of the processes could still run. Trust me. You're going to find your share of these people. You hope you can change their way of thinking. Sometimes you can. The other times, it's like talking to a brick wall."

Our conversation is interrupted by the shuffling of sneakers against the sidewalk. A lanky red-haired high-school boy with a bookbag slung over one shoulder makes his way over to us. I immediately recognize him as Morgan Bender, the oldest child of the Benders, friends of my parents. I've known Morgan all my life.

"Hi, Mr. Paige. Hey, Web," he says, greeting us. "Are you the Oracle?"

He shows me the business card I had just passed out. I glance at my dad who nods, as if to say, "This is your show. Run it."

"Cyber-oracle at your service. What's can I help you with?"

Morgan slides off his bookbag and removes a beaten-up laptop. It's decorated with stickers of bands that I've never heard of before, and likely, my parents would never let me listen to.

"I don't know what happened. One moment I'm working on it, the next, it goes kaplooey."

"Kaplooey?" Vocabulary is not Morgan's strong suit.

"My computer suddenly locked. I can't do anything."

"Hmmm," I muse aloud. "Walk me through what happened. Don't leave out any detail."

"Well, I had bought tickets to a Box of Frogs concert and was going through my emails to see if they had come in. And then I saw a message from some lawyer saying I had inherited some money. To find out more I had to click on a link. So, I clicked on the link. But instead of finding out how to collect the money, my screen was suddenly locked and says I'm in trouble with the FBI."

I share a look with my dad. I can already tell he knows what the problem is, and I think I know too, but I allow Morgan to walk me through everything he did before I offer a recommendation.

"I don't understand how I'm in trouble with the FBI," he adds. The fear in his voice is evident. "I didn't do anything, honest."

"You're not in trouble with the FBI," I tell him. "But you are in trouble with cyber criminals."

"Cyber criminals? How?"

"You've been tricked, Morgan," I say. "It sounds like you've been victimized by ransomware."

"Ransom – what?"

"Malware used to extort money from people like you. What do you think, dad?"

"I think you're spot on, Willy. Keep going."

"Let's look at what we're working with. Please boot up your laptop."

Morgan turns on the laptop. After a moment of noisy processing, a message pops up on the screen with the seal of the Federal Bureau of Investigation emblazoned on it:

Your Computer Has Been Locked! The operating system is locked due to the violation of the federal laws of the United States of America! (Article 1, Section 8, Clause 8; Article 202; Article 210 of the Criminal Code of USA provides for a deprivation of four to twelve years).

To unlock this computer, you are obliged to pay a fine of $500.

You have 72 hours to pay the fine or else you will be arrested. You must pay the fine through this link.

"I don't want to get arrested," Morgan says. "But I don't have that kind of money."

"You aren't going to be arrested. This isn't from the FBI," I say. "Last time, I looked the FBI didn't charge you $500 to give you back access to your own computer."

"But the seal looks legitimate."

"This is how good the bad guys are. They do their homework to make it look legit."

"Are you sure? Because I checked the FBI site and the seal is identical."

"I'm positive. The bad guys are hoping to make you afraid and prey on that fear. Fear of the police. Fear of a fine. And when it comes to ransomware, fear of not being able to get your information back."

"I can't get my information back?"

"Ransomware is a type of malware that restricts your ability to use your computer. Some lock you out like the one you have here. Another type threatens to delete your data. And still another type encrypts your data making you unable to read your files until you pay the ransom."

"Why do they do this?"

My dad speaks up. "To make money. They know that in today's technology-driven lifestyles we all lead, no-one wants to not to be able to get their information. And since most people store all their important information on computers or smartphones, they figure people are willing to pay to get it back."

"I'm so screwed," says Morgan. "My term paper is due in two days and all of my notes and drafts are on there! Can you do anything to help me?"

I bite my lip. Usually with ransomware, unless you have the decrypting key, the files will be inaccessible. But not all criminal gangs are created equal and sometimes the malware is careless and will have a loophole that can be exploited."

I use my smartphone to look up some things regarding the ransomware message, the link attached to the message, and the amount of the ransom. I show this to my father. He understands what I'm looking for and winks at me and nods his head.

Relief swells through me. I turn to Morgan who looks paler than a ghost on Halloween.

"Fortunately, I can with this type of ransomware. If they had encrypted your files, then there would be no way to get at the files in a reasonable amount of time. For this one, I just have to restart the laptop in Safe Mode. Then I open the Internet browser and go to one of the safe sites that have ransomware removal tools like this one. Save the file and run the tool. It will scan the system, identify the ransomware – there it is! Message says it has removed the tool. Now we reboot and see if it worked."

Morgan reboots the machine. The three of us watch with baited breath to see if the machine would return to its former state.

In a few seconds, Morgan's prayers are answered.

"It worked! You saved my butt, Web," Morgan says. "All my files are there."

"You were lucky this time, Morgan," I say. "The malware was sloppy. It wouldn't have worked with other types of malware."

"What can I do to make sure this doesn't happen to me again?"

I turn to my dad.

"Dad?"

"That's a good question………. Safeguarding information is so important. In the past, we used to use safes to keep our valuables secure. When it comes to information, or data, just because we can't hold it per se, there's a tendency not to think about it. Out of sight, out of mind, so to speak. But that doesn't mean that we shouldn't protect it the same way we'd protect our money."

"He's right," I say. "Frequently backing up your information on a removable hard drive such as a USB key is a good way to make sure you can withstand the threat of ransomware or just a simple computer crash."

"Not just ransomware," Dad says. "That's just good hygiene. Sometimes computers just stop working. You've heard of the 'blue screen of death,' haven't you?"

"Yeah."

"When that happens, your hard drive is pretty much dead. And sometimes you can't retrieve your information after."

"I owe you big time," Morgan said. "Now I can finish that paper and graduate to my senior year." Morgan paused. "This was a pretty big job, what's the cost?"

I haven't thought about what the cost of the job should be.

"Favors," I say. "I did a favor for you, you have to do three favors for someone else."

"What kind of favors?"

"Anything you decide."

"How does that sound, Morgan?" my father asks.

"That sounds like I got off pretty cheaply."

43

Chapter Three

That night at dinner, my dad and I plan to eat Chinese take-out, which saves us time in scrubbing burnt pots. I set the table and the doorbell rings.

Dad goes to collect the food. He comes back moments later with a big grin on his face.

"Ping's," he says. "Dinner is served."

At the table, he spoons some chicken lo mein into a bowl and hands it to me, before helping himself to some beef broccoli, extra spicy. He loves broccoli, but I can't stand it. The fuzzy ends feel funny in my mouth. He likes his food spicy, which I don't understand at all. What good is food if you can't even taste it because your mouth feels like a three-alarm fire?

"So, cyber sleuth, how do you feel after solving your first case," he asks, drizzling soy sauce over his food.

I chew thoughtfully for a few moments.

"Excited. Nervous. Both. It's kind of weird," I say. "Is that the way you feel when you are on a case?"

"It never gets boring, I can say that. Each case has its own challenges, its own peculiarities. But that's what helps us solve them. That's why people that like working on puzzles are so good at being investigators. Cyberspace is like one large puzzle in which every computer, every phone, heck, every Internet-connected device are just small pieces."

"That's a lot of pieces," I say.

"That's called job security," he says. "As long as people use computers, there is always going to be the need for people to set them up, to secure them, to fix them, and upgrade them. And you want to know a secret? They're not going away anytime in the future."

"Cool," I say.

After finishing my homework, I call up Tamara. She can't come to the phone because she's still doing her homework. Tamara is such a procrastinator. I don't know how she gets allowed to do anything. I try to contact Josie but she's too busy texting her boy-du-jour. Betta also isn't available.

I walk over to one of my bedroom windows. The sky is already dark and it's not even seven o'clock. In a few weeks it will be Halloween, my favorite time of year. It's like a free holiday for kids – a time when it's encouraged for everyone to be someone else for a night. And the free candy isn't so bad either. Last year, my friends and I did a group costume, meaning we all were dressed up the same way. We were characters from Monster High TV show. This year we are thinking of updating My Pretty Ponies. Although none of us admit to still watching the show, I think we all did.

I love my friends. I've known them since kindergarten. And we have been tight ever since. I'd do anything for them, and them for me.

The rest of the week is kind of slow. No new prospective clients come knocking on my door, and I wonder if my assumption that people have lots of computer problems is off-base. I spend the afternoons on after-school activities, soccer with Tamara and Betta or volunteering to collect and organize canned goods for homeless shelters. By the time Friday rolls around, I'm more than ready for the weekend.

On the Friday bus ride home, I sit next to Josie who is talking about the latest crush she has on a boy. I'm not sure when Josie got into boys. The rest of us are just started to take notice of them. For the longest time they were just other people we used to play with. They weren't so different from us; they liked to run, shout, and avoid their chores whenever they could. Sure, they liked gross things like bugs and fart noises, but that was pretty much to be expected, and came with the territory of them being, well, boys.

But Josie was an early bloomer. She first noticed boys when we were ten, and not just as potential playmates when the rest of the girls were unavailable. She started talking to them differently, with a tone in her voice that she never used when she was talking to us. She also started playing with her hair when she talked to them, making goofy smiley faces.

Now I get it, but back then I just thought she was being weird. My mom said it was puppy love, which I didn't understand considering that boys were boys and not small dogs. But the way my mom seemed so sure of what she was saying, maybe they were.

Anyway, Josie's next to me and talking so fast it's difficult to keep up with what she's saying.

"…I met him at the mall. What are the chances? Right in front of the sports store."

"Oh yeah," I say, trying not to sound too condescending. "Boys just hate sports."

"You know what I mean. Stevie goes to Woodlawn."

I sit upright in my seat.

"Woodlawn is a high school. How old did you say he was?"

"Fifteen. He'll be sixteen in a couple of months." Suddenly, Josie's eyes got wide with excitement. "Oh my God! Can you say driver's license?"

"Wait, wait, wait," I say, trying to recover after that bombshell. "Do you really think talking to a high-school boy is a good idea?"

"What's the big deal? We're just texting."

"Do your parents know?"

"My parents don't care," she says. "They're so busy with their lives, they leave me pretty much alone."

"I don't like it," I say…"Just be careful, ok? Promise me?"

I stick out my pinkie. Josie looks at it and then hooks her pinkie in with mine.

"Promise."

"So, tell me. What's he like? Is he nice?"

"He's better than nice, Web. He's dreamy. Look. Isn't he gorgeous?"

She takes out her pink cell phone and shows me a photograph. The boy has sandy blonde hair that sweeps past blue eyes. He's leaning against a tree with a smirk on his face. He's trying hard to look cool. I automatically don't like him.

"Um, yeah," I say. "He's cute. But isn't he a bit old for you?"

"I'm almost thirteen. My dad is five years older than my mom."

"That's not what I mean, and you know it."

"It's cool, Web. We're just flirting."

"If you say so. What are your plans for the weekend?" I ask, changing the subject.

"Nothing much. Ballet. It's my grandfather's birthday on Saturday. I tried to get out of it, but my mom won't let me."

"What are you talking about? That sounds like it'll be fun."

"Only you would think it's fun watching a bunch of grown-ups sit around a table, playing cards and talking about people you don't know."

Josie knows me too well. I never mind listening when adults are talking. You can hear some interesting things about relatives and sometimes embarrassing stories involving your parents.

The bus pulled over at Josie's stop.

"Later, Gator," she says heading for the door. I wave to her and watch her skip happily to her front door.

Mom's home for dinner marking the first time this week that the three of us are sitting at the kitchen table. It also marks a night that we're eating an honest-to-goodness home-cooked meal. My dad's so relieved he informs my mom that he is going to clean the dishes and every pot and pan used in the making of her famous bacon mac and cheese.

The food is so good no one speaks for a good ten minutes as we hungrily dig into the hot, cheesy, gooey deliciousness.

"How goes the cyber philanthropism?" my mom asks me, taking a break from her plate and washing it down with some cold water.

"Up and down," I say. "It started off busy, but it's cooled down some since."

"Welcome to the business," my father says. "Don't worry. It will pick up and fast. Remember what I'm always saying. There's never a dull moment in cyberspace. The bad guys never sleep."

"I prefer the bad guys in my world," Mom says. "The police usually catch them quickly."

"Well, I've been privileged to get a front-row seat of our daughter in action, Letitia. And I admit, she has some mad skills. She's batting a thousand. Two cases and two happy clients."

"Dad…" I say, rolling my eyes. I try to sound humble, but it always feels good when my dad approves of what I do.

"Just speaking the truth, Willy. I was especially impressed how you helped Morgan Bender. Ransomware is the latest cybercrime tactic that's been targeting everyone. People, police, schools, even hospitals."

"We had training on that this week, especially after that incident in California. The staff has been busy backing up all patient files to make sure we can still do our jobs in case the hospital is victimized by ransomware."

"It works. People still pay the ransom, which gives these criminals incentive to keep using it. Fortunately for Morgan, the attackers that targeted his laptop messed up in the malware code so Willy was able to fix the problem without compromising the information."

"I heard," mom says. "Mrs. Bender called me and told me you saved her son's rear end. Something about a school paper he nearly lost."

"He knows better now," I say.

"I'm proud of you," mom says. "Helping people is a real contribution to the larger community. It's not an easy thing to do. Donating money to a cause or a social issue is always good, but donating time shows a deeper sense of purpose and commitment."

Mom always has a knack for seeing the important things in life.

"Thanks, mom."

Dad stands up and claps his hands loudly together.

"I think this calls for a bookstore trip tomorrow."

"Dad, I didn't do it to get a reward," I remind him.

"Who says you're getting reward? If you're going to embark on this cyber security crusade, you're going to need the tools to do it. There are two books off the top of my head that you are going to need to read."

That night in bed, I take out a spiral notebook from the nightstand drawer. I open it and write in Morgan Bender's name underneath Mrs. Okafur. Then I write the dates, the nature of their problem, and how they were resolved. It's only two names, and they look awfully small in the empty lined space around them. But that's okay. Every journey starts with a first step.

These are my steps.

And my journey has just begun.

Turn the Page Books is my favorite bookstore in town. It's a large two-level store that has just about every book you can imagine. They have a daily story time hour where parents with young children can come and listen to one of the employees read Dr. Seuss and other popular kids' books.

It's difficult not to wander the aisles because there are so many books that I want to read. Every section has something different for me. Fiction provides me the necessary mental escape and a balance from the more left-brain reading that I'm drawn to. Psychology tests my comprehension of the human side of people's motivations and activities, and poetry soothes my right-brain cravings.

But my favorite sections are science and true crime. Technology excites me because it introduces me to new inventions that will be coming out. Turn the Page Books boasts a generous information technology section, mainly because the Washington, D.C. area has a bustling IT sector.

I'm flipping through a hardcover book on hacking techniques when my father's voice startles me.

"Find anything interesting?" he asks. I see he already has four books under his own arm. My father is such a bibliophile. Books for him are like player memorabilia for sports fans.

"Too many things," I lament. "There are like a dozen books I want to buy."

My father laughs.

"The only thing is you have to find time to read them all."

Boy, wasn't that the truth. I don't understand when people say they don't like to read. There is literally something for everyone, every like, every interest. How do you not want to learn more about a subject that interests you?

I must have that look I get when I'm trying to solve a difficult problem, because my father's expression changes. I don't know when I'm doing it. I just have to see someone's reaction to know I'm doing it.

"Spill it, Willy," he says good-naturedly.

"I'm kind of embarrassed." After getting such praise from my father for helping Morgan with his computer problem, it seems almost hypocritical to ask him a question.

"There are no dumb questions," he says. "Only silly people who don't ask when they have them."

"Okay, but don't laugh. What is the Internet of Things? I mean, I get the big picture – it references everything that connects to the Internet, but it doesn't make sense that refrigerators are connected to the Internet."

"That's not a dumb question at all. And to tell you the truth, even the experts are still wrapping their minds around it because it's still a relatively new and emerging concept. 'Things' refers to exactly what you think – any device, any watch, TV, car even, anything that can connect to the Internet is considered part of the Internet of Things. And all that means is that these devices can be controlled remotely. So, if you want to set your house lights to turn on at a specific hour, they will. If you want a reminder to pick up some milk before you get home, you can set your refrigerator to not only remind you but send in an order to your store."

"That's a lot of devices," I say. "It certainly sounds like that could really make people's lives easier."

"There's definitely that possibility. That's why many people are excited about it. Most people like it when their lives can be simplified by technology."

I recognize the tone in my father's voice that tells me there's a catch.

"But…" I say.

"But, as often is the case, so much focus is put on developing the technology to make it faster and user friendly that the manufacturers forget about the security aspects of it. Security is an afterthought."

"Really? Even today when there's so many news stories about hackers and criminals exploiting networks and stealing everything from personal information to corporate trade secrets?"

My dad laughs.

"I forget how in touch you are with what's going on in the world. If only the bigwigs at companies had your understanding," he says. "But to be fair, companies just started taking cyber security seriously. For a long time, as long as it didn't impact the bottom line, they were okay with it. But when they found out that large losses of information and research and customer data make them look bad in the public eye, they started to take notice. Unfortunately, in most cases, by the time security is considered, the product is already developed, sold, and purchased."

"That's horrible," I say.

"Your generation will be the ones to make things better. For now, our leaders in Washington barely know how to use computers, no less try to figure out a way to better secure them. But that's for another lesson."

He peruses the shelves of books in front of us. He finds what he's looking for and pulls it out.

"This should catch you up to speed."

The book screams out in big black letters – THE INTERNET OF THINGS!!!!

So much for subtlety.

One of our favorite things to do after we buy new books is to go to the nearby park and sit on a bench, get some hotdogs, and read. The park is always a good place to go to sit and people watch. There's a swing and slides, plenty of park benches, and a small pond where ducks float and eat bread pieces thrown to them by the public. My dad goes to a nearby hotdog vendor to get us some snacks while I find a good bench with shade.

Before I can crack open my new book, my dad comes over and hands me a plain hot dog, chips, and a soda. He sits down next to me with a heavy plop and starts to dig into his "works" – a hot dog that is literally smothered in every condiment and fixing on the vendor's hand cart. He likes his food sloppy, which is probably the reason why many of his shirts have discolorations from spills and droppings that he haphazardly tried to wipe away.

Sitting next to us are two mothers – one black hair the other blonde – who watch their children play among a throng of kids crawling over a jungle gym. The black-haired woman looks to be in her early thirties and drinks coffee out of an oversized travel mug. I don't usually try to eavesdrop on anyone's conversation, but these two talk loud.

"How are you holding up?" she asks the blonde woman who looks to be the same age as the brunette. She wears a baggy and paint-stained University of Virginia sweatshirt.

"Domenico is a cutie," the black hair woman says, "but he is such a handful. Twenty months old and there's nothing he doesn't get into or put into his mouth."

"And your daughter, Lucy?"

"She's with daddy. She's five months next week. Sweet as sugar that one."

"There is a difference between girls and boys, I swear you would think they didn't come from the same parents," the blonde says. "My Elizabeth is five years old and about as perfect as a five-year-old can be. Her brother, on the other hand, is two and living up to the 'terrible' moniker. Plus, he's colicky. They make a bad combination."

"You know, I have to say," the black-haired woman says. "I'm just happy with the new stuff they're coming out with. We got a baby monitor with a camera as well as a microphone. It's such a relief to be able to see little Lucy sleep instead of popping our heads in every two seconds when she makes a noise. Even if we're outside for something, we can just bring up the feed on our phones."

"You have one of those? I've heard they can be dangerous," the blonde woman comments.

"What do you mean? How can a baby monitor be dangerous? It's not like I put it in the crib with my daughter."

"My sister has one. Well, let's just say something weird happened."

The black-haired woman's face becomes alarmed.

"What do you mean?"

"Listen to this. Last month after she put down her son for a nap, she started to tidy up the room. And then she heard someone speak to her."

"Who? Was someone in the room?"

"Not physically at least. But the voice scared her. What he was saying."

"What kind of things?" asks the dark-haired woman. The hints of concern in her voice are unmistakable.

The blonde woman looks around self-consciously.

"Someone was calling her baby ugly and making strange noises. It was coming from the baby monitor."

"It must have been a crossed signal or something. I mean, it's not like he saw her, right? That's impossible."

"I don't know. The guy was saying things that only my sister could see. She ended up unplugging the monitor and then the harassment stopped."

I look up from my book. I haven't been reading since I started listening to the conversation, but I didn't want to look like I was being a nosy busybody. Chewing my lip, I think about the details. Internet-connected baby monitor. Things like security settings immediately jump to the forefront. A cross-connection is always possible. But when the "crossed" signal has somebody describing a baby's blanket and stuffed animals, that's not a coincidence.

I glance at my father who has been watching me the whole time. I can tell he's been listening too. Our eyes meet as if to say, "I know what happened."

"Should I say something?" I ask him.

"If you don't, I will," he says. That's all the prompting I need.

"Excuse me," I say, rising to my feet and walking over to the two women. "I don't mean to eavesdrop, and I'm sorry to interrupt, but that wasn't a crossed signal."

The two women share a look. I'm sure they never expected a twelve-year old girl to be telling them what actually happened no less solving the case at hand.

"What do you mean?" asked the dark headed lady.

"You said that you could access the video feed on your smart phone."

"Yes. All video monitors do that."

I let that statement sit and turn to the blonde.

"Your sister's model has that capability too I take it?" I ask her.

"Yes," she replies. "She could do that too. Why is that important?"

"It's simple. It wasn't a cross-signal that was coming from the microphone. Someone had hacked into your sister's baby monitor."

"That's crazy. That sounds like something from a movie."

"It does," I say. "And it does happen."

"But…how?"

"Smart baby monitors, like the one your sister has, pass live feeds through a user's wireless router and over the Internet. The good news is that enables you to view it remotely on a smartphone or tablet or laptop. The bad news is, if you don't have the proper security in place on your home Wi-Fi and on the monitor, they are susceptible to be broken into by the bad guys."

"That sounds so confusing," says the dark-haired lady.

"It's not really. You have Wi-Fi at home, correct?" I ask.

"Correct," says the dark-haired lady.

"Is it secured?"

"I don't really know," she admitted to Web.

"Securing your home Wi-Fi is important particularly as the Internet of Things becomes a reality. In the not-so-distant future, everything will be able to be accessed via the Internet. But it's also important that you ensure that these devices don't have their security settings set to default. For that you just have to check the device and change the setting."

"But how do we make our home Wi-Fi safe?" the blonde asks. "I mean, I'm not a computer whiz or anything. I just don't know about that stuff."

"Me neither," adds the dark-haired woman.

"Well, there are several steps you can take. First, make sure encryption is enabled. Most routers come out of the box with encryption turned off. Second, make sure that the router's firewall is turned on. Three, change default passwords on the router. Most wireless routers come with preset passwords. The bad guys know this and will test to see if these are in place. Four, change the router's service set identifier, or SSID. This is the name of your in-house network. It's a good thing to make it innocuous. Turning off the broadcast of the SSID is a good thing too to keep you more private. Last, use the Media Access Control address to filter any device trying to connect to your network."

The women look at me with blank, lost expressions. I have to remember not to get too far into the weeds when it comes to technology and let the knowledge of the individual guide me on how I'm explaining things.

"I'm sorry, but I don't know if I'll be able to do all of that," the dark-haired woman says finally. "That's a lot of technical things to remember, and I was a Classics major in college. Latin yes, numbers no."

"Don't worry," I tell her. "I'd be happy to help out."

And with that, I remove two business cards from my jeans' pocket. I hand one to each of the women.

The dark-haired woman smiles.

"Now, Oracle is something that I can understand," she says. "You have that insight?"

"I'm trying to. My dad is the real Oracle," I say, gesturing over to my dad on the park bench. He waves at us. "He's a computer forensics expert."

"Well, I feel like I'm in good hands," the blonde says.

"If you want, I'd be happy to come over some time and take a look at your Wi-Fi setup. It'll be easy."

"Great. I'll give you a call tomorrow."

"Great," I say. I start to head back to my father.

"One more question," the blonde asks. "How much do you charge?"

"This is easy. Two favors."

"I'm sorry. Did you say favors?"

"Yep. Next time someone asks you for help, give it to them. Doesn't have to be big. Just do something nice for someone who needs it."

The dark-haired woman breaks into a big smile.

"I wish more people did what you're doing. That's sending some positive energy into the world."

"That's the plan. See you!"

I head over to my father who sees the two women waving at us.

"I think you made a good impression," he says.

"They need help."

My dad reaches out and grabs me in a headlock and nuggies my head playfully.

"Hey what's that for?" I squeal. I love it when my dad shows more of his spontaneous personal side. Sometimes he can come across as being too reserved. Mom says he was a prankster in college even though I have never seen any of these clownish qualities.

"A favor for a favor," he says. "I'm paying it forward."

"Dad!"

Chapter Four

Monday morning brings a never-ending wave of rain. It started late last night and continued.

This is beyond cats and dogs level.

This is something more on the Biblical level.

My mom quickly takes the plates off the table and dumps them into the kitchen sink.

"Make sure you bring an umbrella," she tells me. "Doesn't look like it's going to let up anytime soon."

"Great," I say.

Rain is the one thing I can't stand when it comes to weather. You can still go out in any other weather condition. The heat and humidity are always manageable, and if it gets too much, you can always escape it by going indoors into some air conditioning. And if it snows, well, you can have snowball fights or go sledding or make snow angels. But there's nothing you can do in the rain but get wet shoes and socks and have a parent mad at you for tracking mud inside.

"When I was your age…"

"I know, I know. Barefoot. Ten miles to school one way. Got it."

My father laughs at the table.

"She has you there," he says to my mother.

"Cornelius? Hush," she says, taking a final sip of her coffee.

Moments later, the school bus groans its way down our street.

"I believe your ride is here, Willy," my father says. He rises and helps me into my red ladybug raincoat. Mom hands me my lunch and umbrella.

"Love you!"

"Love you too!"

I don't see Josie on the bus, and I wonder if she's sick or if her mom is giving her a ride to school. Yesterday, I helped Brigid and Maria (the blonde and dark-haired woman from the park) better secure their home Wi-Fi accesses. First, I changed the names of their home networks and told them to change it on a quarterly basis. Next, I also changed their passwords, and ensured their encryption was activated. I did a couple of other things as well, like turning off guest networks (routers offer a mode that creates a separate network for guests) and stressed the need to use virtual private networks (which are ways that add security and privacy).

Both women were very grateful and promised to do their part in making this world a better place. Brigid is a physical therapist and her friend Maria is a professor of Spanish at one of the universities in Washington, D.C. I told them that they had the perfect jobs already to help others.

My first three periods go by in a blur. My math and science classes are broken up with art and happen to be my favorite three classes. Afternoon classes are a bit rougher with history, English, and Spanish. After lunch, I have a free period and usually head to the library to do some research or help Mrs. Gibson, the librarian, sort return books or restock them on the shelves. As you see, I really can't get enough of books.

At lunch, my friends and I continue to discuss what we're going to be for Halloween. What starts as a brainstorming session invariably turns into a gripe session about homework, teachers, or something someone's parent did over the weekend.

Josie is preoccupied with her phone as always.

"Give it a rest already," Tamara says to Josie. "We're right here, who could you be texting?"

"You're just jealous," Josie says.

"Don't tell me you're still talking to that Woodlawn clown," Tamara says. Looks like Josie shared her new infatuation among our group.

"Whatever," Josie says. "Anybody get that last question on the quiz on Friday?"

I look at Josie. She's back looking at her phone without caring to hear the response. Sometimes I think she talks just so that she can be heard.

After lunch, I make my way to the library. A complete wall of windows reveals that the rains onslaught hasn't let up, pouring down the plate glass in steady streams. I groan out loud. I swear, if it keeps on raining someone is going to have to build an ark.

The library is fuller than usual because no one can hang outside in between classes. Some read, but most are chatting in hushed whispers, cracking jokes and trying to cover their laughter. I feel bad for the kids trying to get in some quiet time.

Libraries for me are special places. I find them comforting and welcoming. Despite all the information available on the Internet, reading a book is always more personal than scrolling through pages on a PDF on the computer. I think it has something to do with the touch. There are so many books on so many topics, you can immerse yourself in and go to a different place and time. Like bookstores, libraries are a home away from home.

One time I took a bus to the public library and the driver chuckled when he saw where I was going.

"I didn't think kids even knew what a library was anymore," he said.

I proudly showed him my well-worn plastic card.

"My library card isn't just for looks, you know," I informed him.

I make my way over to Mrs. Gibson's desk. Librarians are the best kept secret in libraries. People think they're mean but they are actually very resourceful. Often Mrs. G has helped me get hard-to-find books relevant to my research projects and papers. She always has helpful tricks of the librarian trade, ready to direct me in a particular direction, or else roll up her own sleeves and lend a hand. That's why I'm always willing to pitch in when I can.

Mrs. G is looking more frantic than usual. She's always under-staffed, inundated with too many tasks and too little hands to get them done.

"Hey, Mrs. G," I say setting my books on the desk. "What can I help you with today?"

"The real question, Web," she answers, "Is what I don't need help with. I have almost two weeks of returns that need to be checked in and restocked. I have ten boxes of donations to cull through, not to mention I need to start thinking about our Fall for the Book festival, which is one month away."

I don't know how much Mrs. G makes, but it certainly isn't enough. I spy a bunch of books that need to be re-shelved.

"I'll do this in a jiff," I say, grabbing the cart and pushing it to the stacks.

I head to the back of the room and start re-shelving books in the reference section. I have to remind myself of the task at hand and not get distracted flipping through the pages of some of the more interesting titles. Encyclopedias may not be as "vogue" as their Wikipedia digital counterpart, but they are no less interesting to bibliophiles like me.

The final reference book I return is the latest iteration of Hacking Uncovered, a series that teaches security practitioners the techniques of hackers and how to defend against them. It's nice to see another kid is interested in this stuff.

A loud sigh captures my attention. I turn to see Mr. Hunter, the school's music teacher, sitting in front of one of the computers that the library provides. He stares intently at the screen so hard, you'd think he was trying to bore holes through it.

Another heavy sigh means he's got a problem. A computer problem.

"Something the matter, Mr. Hunter?" I ask him.

"I'm afraid so, Web," he says. He takes off his glasses and rubs his eyes with his fingers. He looks way stressed.

"My laptop is moving at a snail's pace. I know technology keeps getting better and more advanced every day, but this is only three months old. It's driving me absolutely crazy!"

"Hmmmmm," I muse aloud. "You're right. It's not outdated – yet. How much memory do you have on it?"

"I don't know. Whatever came with the machine?"

Mr. Hunter fumbles around the keyboard. I can tell he needs some help.

"I think I can give you a hand, Mr. Hunter. Mind if I take a look?"

Mr. Hunter pushes the laptop over to me.

"Please do. I'm afraid I'm not technologically gifted, you might say."

"No worries." I take the opportunity to pass him my business card."

Mr. Hunter checks out the card and raises his eyebrows.

"Oracle, eh? Well, tell you what, Web. If you can get this back to the way it used to be, I'll herald your exploits like a Greek chorus."

I laugh.

"That's a deal," I say.

I check the laptop's task manager. That's just the program that lets you know what processes and applications are running on the computer. Then I check to see how much disk space is available, as well as the computer's memory. The total processor utilization for the laptop is maxed out at 100 percent.

"Huh," I say.

"What is it? Do I have a virus?"

"Here's your problem," I say, turning the laptop so Mr. Hunter can see. "This is indicative of either a virus or spyware. Have you updated your antivirus?"

"I usually do it once a week," Mr. Hunter says. "I was going to do it tomorrow."

"First and foremost. To be on the safe side, you should update every day. It takes just a minute or so and can make the difference between being protected or getting slammed with the latest malware."

I start the antivirus update. While it loads, I look at the cook books on the table.

"These yours?"

"Yes," he says. "I have to make something for the teacher's fundraiser this month. Unfortunately, the last thing I cooked was a microwave dinner."

"I see." This gets me thinking. "So, can I ask you what you were researching?"

"Sure. I was researching recipes. I found a bunch of sites and started perusing them and bookmarking those pages that had some things that I think even I could make."

"Do you download the recipes?"

"Of course. I hate to print out things if I don't need to. I try to be very environmentally conscious."

"That's good to hear," I say. "But I think you've found the root of your problem here. See, sometimes you can get bad things by where you go online and what you do when you get there. For example, spyware usually ends up on computers because you clicked a button on a pop-up window. It automatically installs a software package to your Web browser."

"What kind of package?"

"The bad kind."

"Wow, I didn't know that," says Mr. Hunter. "So, someone is spying on me?"

"Well, yes and no," I tell him. "Technically, spyware is a form of adware. Adware refers to a type of software that once installed on your computer will send you pop-up ads or redirect your browser to other web sites."

"Now that you mention it," says Mr. Hunter, "I have noticed lately when I've typed in an address to the URL, it sends me someplace else. I always thought I was fat-fingering my typing."

"Not always. Adware for the most part is looking for information like what sites you visit, and not after more valuable things like sensitive personal information. But the bad guys have also been known to use spyware for those purposes as well."

Mr. Hunter shakes his head.

"I don't know what to say. What do you think? Can you help me out or do I need to get a new computer? I'd hate to lose all my research because of this. I keep all of the music I write on this bucket of bolts."

I want to tell Mr. Hunter that there are no bolts in laptops but decide against it. I check the antivirus program. It's now updated.

"Let's see where we are at," I say. "We're going to run a scan and see what happens. It's also a good thing to periodically run security scans."

Mr. Hunter eyes the screen as the scan bar commences. He stares at the bar as if to make the scan go faster. I try to ease his concerns.

"Staring at it won't make it go faster," I say.

"I know," he says. "I'm just so worried."

"The scan will detect the problem if its known. That's why frequent antivirus updates and running scans are so important."

"And you're sure it will detect it?"

"As long as it's known to the antivirus software companies, they more often than not have a security signature that will detect it."

"How often do you update your antivirus?"

"Not frequent enough," he says.

"You'd be surprised how many people realize that. Usually when it's too late. Hopefully, this is an easy fix."

"I won't make that mistake again," he says.

"You'd be surprised how many people say that as well," I say. "Now, another way you can look for spyware is go to the Control Panel and check your list of installed programs for items that you don't remember installing or using. There will generally be a lot of programs on the list and it's possible that the spyware will be shown here. If you see a program that you didn't specifically want, uninstall it."

"That sounds difficult," Mr. Hunter laments.

"So, does a C-Minor scale."

The scan concludes. It registered the presence of spyware on the laptop.

"Is that bad?"

"Bad in the fact that you have spyware, but good in the fact that we found it. And here's your culprit."

I point at the antivirus scanner's notification banner prompting the removal of the infected files that it had detected.

"And you definitely want to do this."

I show Mr. Hunter how to click "YES" and the antivirus program removes the questionable files. I ask permission to save all of Mr. Hunter's documents while I'm here, and he immediately agrees.

"Ok," I say. "Reboot the computer and it should work a lot faster."

Mr. Hunter follows instruction well. When the laptop comes back up, it is noticeably quicker.

"Web!" he exclaims, soliciting a stink-eye from Mrs. G. "You are a lifesaver! I'm so lucky to have run into you today."

"No prob, Mr. H," I say. "Just doing my job."

"I'll keep this handy," he says, sliding my business card into his pocket.

"Now, sometimes, the more aggressive spyware hides itself with more care," I tell him. That's why it's always good to run a program specifically designed to find this type of malware. Just make sure it works with your antivirus program. You don't want to cause problems where there are none."

"And you can help me with that?"

"Yes, I can help you with that."

He sits back, removing a handkerchief from his back pocket and wiping his forehead.

"Your card says that pay depends on the job. How would you and your family like to attend a fall concert at the Spectrum as my guests? It's the least I can do."

"That sounds really good," I say. 'But I usually ask that people do a favor for someone else as payment."

Mr. Hunter looks impressed.

"I like that," he says. "Tell you what. I'll bring one of the classes to the concert as a cultural field trip."

"That would be awesome! I say. "Consider the payment remunerated."

Tamara, Betta, and I line up for afternoon soccer practice. We're running sprints as a team punishment for our lackluster play in our last game. Coach Wind patrols up and down with a big silver whistle in his mouth.

"Okay, ladies!" he shouts and blows the whistle.

The first line of girls sprint to the mid-field, touch the line, and head back. T, Betta, and I share a look. We are not huge fans of running, although Betta is the fastest on the team. You'd think she'd like running more but she doesn't.

"Anyone see Josie this weekend? I texted her twice and never got a response," I say to my friends as the next line of girls hustle off their marks and head to mid-field.

"She's been hanging with that boy," Betta says. She digs her cleats into ground when she sees our teammates race toward us.

"Who?" I ask. Like I said before, it's difficult to keep up with her social life.

"Ready! Go!" Coach Wind shouts. The shrill of the whistle is like ice running along my spine.

My question goes unanswered as we run. Betta takes an early lead. She runs so effortlessly, she's the envy of many girls on the team. She's reached mid-field before the next fastest girl is even close to the line. I flash a quick grin at T. We always have a friendly competition in whatever we do. It can be drinking chocolate milk, running, doing an art project, whatever.

We reach the mid-line almost at the same time.

"Slow poke!" she says. She's sucking some serious air.

"Catch me if you can," I say.

We run all-out for the end-line. My arms pump madly. Betta's already made it back. We both are laughing as we sprint. Neither one of us wants to lose bragging rights.

We cross neck and neck. I sure wish someone was taking pictures, because this is definitely a photo-finish. I'm pretty sure I beat T, but she insists that she had me by a nose.

"Well?" We both look at Betta to settle the dispute. "Who won?"

Betta looks at T, then me. Her face is difficult to read, although I'm pretty sure she will see the result as I do.

She suddenly shrugs her shoulders and retrieves her soccer ball for the next skill set.

"I don't know," she says. "I wasn't paying attention."

T and I look at each other and groan. Betta is such the diplomat when it comes to her friends.

"Come on," she says. "It's the shoot around!"

On the bus home that afternoon, I ask Tamara about Josie. She checks her phone.

"You know, the boy at Woodlawn," she says. "She was at the mall with him again this weekend."

"He's too old for her," I say. "She shouldn't hang around boys like that."

"I'm with you," T says. "But you know how she is. She always thinks she's more mature than she is. I'm hoping that she gets over it soon."

"Yeah, but what if she doesn't? What then?"

"I don't know. Maybe it will work out. He'll get bored of her. I mean, he's practically driving now, right? What could he see in Josie?"

"I'm not so sure. And that's what worries me."

"It'll be okay, Web. Josie's a good girl."

"Yeah," I say. "Maybe you're right."

It's easier to say than believe. I just hope my imagination is not over-hyper like it does sometimes. My mother says my imagination is what makes me very creative, and my dad says it helps me better at looking at things from a different perspective. But right now, it just makes me concerned for my friend.

After dinner, I wash the dishes while my father dries and stacks. Although he is not such a great cook, he cleans with precision. I don't mind washing dishes because it gives me time to think. I get to work through problems in my head and really get to the nitty-gritty. The situation with Josie is turning me into knots. I'm so engrossed in trying to figure out how to approach her again, that I barely see my father take some soap suds and put it on my head.

"I'd say a penny for your thoughts, but the way you're chomping down on your lip, I'm not sure I could afford them," he says.

I crack a half-smile. My father can always get me to laugh.

"Sorry," I say. "I was just thinking about something."

"Clearly," he says. "I don't need to be Sherlock Holmes to figure that out. Care to share, or is it strictly hush-hush?"

I'm lucky because my parents are always very respectful of my friends. They never force me to betray their trust or confidence. Hush-hush is his way of asking if it's a pinkie-swear level secret or something that can be discussed.

"Well," I say, chewing it over for a second. "It's not hush-hush. I don't know if there's really anything there to be honest. It has to do with Josie. And a boy."

His eyebrows arch.

"Ah," he says, like he's just solved a mystery. "Boys. Any insight I can provide? You know, I used to be a boy."

I give him a look like he's crazy.

"Josie likes this boy that I don't think she should like."

"Do you like the boy?"

I made a face.

"Gross. I don't like boys. And I don't even know this one."

Now it is my father's turn to look confused.

"Ok," he says. "You lost me. Don't you go to the same school?"

"We do," I say. "The boy doesn't. He goes to a different school. Woodlawn."

"Woodlawn is a high school," he says.

"And that's the point," I say.

My father makes a face like someone has just splashed ice cold water in his face. He takes a few seconds as he formulates his next question.

"And this boy is dating Josie?"

"Yes. No. I don't know. They saw each other at the mall this past weekend. Am I being too protective of my friend?"

"That's not for me to say," he says. "I understand your trepidation. He's what – fifteen, sixteen?"

"Fifteen," I say.

He pulls on his chin with his fingers like he does when he works through his own problems.

"Talk to her. See what it's about. Maybe it's just a friend thing. Maybe it's not. But if you judge her before you know what she's thinking or feeling, you may drive her away from you."

"Talk," I reiterate.

"Conversation. It's the cornerstone of society."

In bed, I write Mr. Hunter's name in my ledger. It feels good to help people. Being able to make a difference in someone's life, there's nothing like it.

I just wish I could do the same for Josie.

Chapter Five

Thursday at recess, I find Josie watching a bunch of kids play four-square. Four-square is serious business at school. There's always a line of people trying to get in. Cory Lewis is king at the game and always controls the flow of the action. Josie has been wanting to beat Cory for a long time. She almost did it last week, but he got her out on a technicality.

"Whatssup player!" I say, approaching her. "Is this going to be the rematch of the century?"

Josie turns to me and shakes her head.

"Web," she says. "What in the world was that?"

"I'm breaking in a new thing," I say. "Does it work?"

"I'd leave that phrase to the real players," she says. "And yeah, today is payback."

She says it loud enough for Cory to hear her. He slams the rubber ball hard and bounces too high for the Maggie Shimkus to bat it back.

"Dream on, Josie," he says. "Next!"

"We haven't seen you the past two weekends," I say to Josie. "We have a costume to come up with, or did you forget?"

"Oh," she says. "I'll do whatever everyone wants to do."

"You usually have a strong opinion when it comes to costumes," I remind her. "Monster High was totally your idea and it killed."

"I just have my mind on other things," she says.

"Are any of those things named Stevie?"

She glances away from me.

"Maybe," she says. "We spend a lot of time at the mall. We play video games or see a movie. On Sunday he bought me an ice cream."

"Sounds like a regular romance," I say.

"That's not funny," she says. "I like him. And he likes me. What's the big deal?"

"His age."

"Drop it, Web. It's none of your business."

"You're right. It's not. I care about you. I want you to be safe."

"I am safe. He hasn't done anything inappropriate, ok?"

"Would you tell me if he did?"

"Yes."

"Sister-promise?" I say, sticking out my pinkie.

She smiles.

"Sister-promise," she says. We interlock pinkies and go through a series of hand moves, our signature secret handshake.

The rest of the school day is pretty much the usual routine of classes, gossiping, and finally concluding on what the group will be for Halloween-. My Little Pony characters. It's the easiest to do as we each have our favorite characters. Tamara is all about Rainbow Dash. Betta is into Twilight Sparkle. Josie, despite her preoccupation with boys, has a soft spot for Fluttershy, and I will be Applejack. Picking the character is one thing; getting a costume to fit the theme is another. In this regard, T is ahead of the game already finding a rainbow wig and skirt.

After lunch, I help one of my teachers, Mrs. Stutz, upgrade the software in the school's computer lab. Ten computers needed an immediate upgrade of operating systems, as the old ones were no longer being serviced by the company that made them. That means, the company was not going to create patches for holes in the code since they had newer, more up-do-date versions that people use.

I don't necessarily consider it one of my Oracle-esque jobs as much as an emergency need for the school. Like I've said, it's surprising to see how many adults can't perform basic computer tasks, like installing software or upgrading operating systems. The more people can do the most basic computer-related fixes and upgrades, the better they will be able to not just solve problems but take care of their own online security.

Mrs. Stutz stands over me as I work my way down the line.

"I don't know what I'd do if you weren't here today, Web," she says. "Mr. Stearns usually takes care of all the technical mumbo-jumbo and he's been out all week on vacation."

"Glad to be of assistance," I say. "These operating systems were really old."

"We didn't have it in the budget until this year. You know what this month is, right?"

I glance at the calendar on the wall. It's the third day of October. Halloween is at the end of the month, but I don't think she means that.

Then it hits me.

Duh, it's cyber security month! The Department of Homeland Security started Cyber Security Month in 2004 as way of raising public awareness about the importance of cyber security. It emphasizes the point that cyber security is not just about having better technology and upgrading making sure computers have security patches in place, but it's also about people getting better educated on the nature of cyber threats and how the bad guys try to trick you.

"I should have known that," I say. Sometimes I get scramble brained.

"Next week, Principal McKerrick will have an assembly on it. Do you want to speak? You can provide the youth perspective."

I like the idea. It totally fits into my new role of being an Oracle for all computer users.

"Definitely! Thank you, Mrs. Stutz!"

"Thank you, Web. Now, we don't have to temporarily close the computer lab. You saved the day!"

"Business is booming!" I announce proudly as I enter the kitchen.

Mom puts away clean dishes. My father sits at his end of the table writing checks to pay bills.

"Glad to hear it," my mom says, handing me three glasses to put in the cabinet near the door.

"I sure wish you were getting paid in dollars," my father says. "Did you take a look at this water bill?"

"Ha-ha," I say as I place the glasses in the cabinet.

"Oh, hush now, Cornelius," my mother says. "You should be proud of your daughter."

"I am proud of her. So, what's the count as of today?" he asks me.

I sit across from my father at the table.

"Clients or favors?"

"Both."

"Five happy customers, seventeen favors."

"That's not bad at all. But tell me. How can you be so sure that the people will follow through and do the favors you ask of them?"

"Always the pessimist, Cornelius," my mother playfully scolds her father. "Don't you listen to him, honey. People are good at heart."

"Your mother's right, Willy. You've done a good job helping people and that needs to be recognized."

"How about we recognize it at the Tastee Cream?" I suggest. The Tastee Cream is my favorite place to get hamburgers and ice cream.

"And she's a tough negotiator."

"She gets that from my side of the family," my mom says, smirking.

At the Tastee Cream, my dad brings back our orders from the counter. I get my usual – hamburger, sweet potato fries, and a chocolate milk shake. Dad gets a chili dog and fried okra (disgusting!) and a coffee. Mom gets a chili dog and a diet soda.

"Your mom's right, Willy," he says. "You're doing good things helping people improve their computer situations. Cyber security month is not enough to carry people through the whole year. I think we're getting better as a society, but the progress is moving too slowly to keep up with the speed at which the bad guys are operating. Millions and millions of financial information is stolen each year, and people still don't think it's going to happen to them."

He pauses to take a big bite of his chili dog. Like at the park, Dad's hotdog is buried in fixings. Only this time it's chili. A lot of it slops down the sides of his mouth as his teeth come down in a bite.

"I read that $15 billion was stolen from businesses in the United States just last year," my mother says, "and that nearly 17 million U.S. citizens were the victim of identity theft the year before."

"And that number is only going to get higher. The world isn't going to be less connected in the future. People have to understand that organizations can only do so much and that they have to watch out for their own security."

I nod thoughtfully. My dad is right. People need to do their part in making sure that the bad guys don't always win. Even if a business, or any person really, could completely secure their networks, it would do little good if people didn't maintain stringent passwords, frequently update their antivirus, and ensure that all known vulnerabilities were patched on their home computers.

"Cornelius? Cornelius Paige, is that you?"

All three of our heads turn to see Justin Ransom, a friend of my father's, standing with a large bag of take-out in his hand.

"Justin Ransom, how the heck are you? It's been a dog's age since I've seen you. You remember my wife, Letitia, and daughter, Willy."

Mr. Ransom gives each of us a nod.

"You'll excuse me, my hands are full," he says. He looks at me and shakes his head. "Willy, you are growing like a weed, young lady. You all need to bottle what you're feeding her and sell it. Make it a million."

I can't help but smile and blush. Mr. Ransom is the type of adult who always inadvertently embarrasses you publicly with compliments.

"How is your family?" my mother asks. "Your son Matthew graduated last June, didn't he? What's he doing for work now?"

Justin sighs heavily. He eyes the spare chair.

"You mind if I take a seat?"

"Take a load off, Justin," my father says.

Justin sits in the empty chair next to my dad.

"I don't know, Letitia, where do I begin? He had a promising job interview with a firm last week. He got down to the final two, but they went with the other candidate."

"I'm sorry to hear it," my mother says. "I wouldn't worry about it too much. I'm sure he will get something soon."

"Well, that's just it, Letitia. This was the third time he made it to the finals and each time the organization went with the other person. I don't understand it. I checked his resume myself. He dresses appropriately for the interviews. We even rehearse questions beforehand."

"That is frustrating," my father says. "I'm sorry to hear it, Justin."

That must be annoying, I think. It sounds like he's doing everything he can. I can see not getting one or maybe even two of the positions, but everyone that he is up for? Something seems off. My father sees me chewing my lip and knows I have something stewing in my brain.

"I know that look," he says. "What's on your mind, Willy?"

"Well, it just seems strange that three times Matt makes it to the final two but doesn't get selected. Two is a coincidence, more than that is a pattern. From what I'm hearing, he's got all the qualifications that separate him from the pack. So, I'm thinking that there is something else causing potential employers to look the other way. Figure that out, and I think you'll have your answer."

Justin looks at my father who just arches his eyebrows.

"Cornelius?" he says to my dad.

"She has a knack at looking at things," he says. "I'd hear what she has to say."

"I'm all ears," says Justin, turning his full attention to me. "Anything you can think of that could help me figure this out, I'd be in your debt."

I dig into my backpack and remove my Tablet and start it up.

"I was reading an article the other day about how social media has been a boon. Not just for people, but for job recruiters."

"You read that?" Justin asks incredulously.

"She reads everything," my father says. "Willy has her fingers on the pulse of technology."

"A chip off the old block, eh, Cornelius," Justin says.

"Not her," my father says. "She's better."

I smile and shake my head. My father is crazy sometimes.

I bring up a search engine and pull up a few articles in a couple of windows.

"See?" I say to Mr. Ransom, showing him the screen. "Recruiters are not only using social media to help them find the kind of candidates they're looking for, but also to weed out the ones that they don't want to have."

A strange look creeps across Mr. Ransom's face.

"What do you mean?" he asks leaning in closer.

"More than half of employers use candidate's social media profiles and accounts as a screening mechanism. So, when they have a candidate, they'll research his social media presence, reviewing all accounts that person has, to see what kind of behavior they demonstrate and if that might make the company look bad."

"What would a social media profile, or whatever you call it, tell a recruiter?" Mr. Ransom asks.

"There are several reasons they check social media. If it's a professional social media site like LinkedIn, the recruiter may find a candidate's published work or mutual connections that can further corroborate a candidate's capabilities. For others, the types of material that is shared – photos, posts, videos – that may help them decide if this is the type of candidate they want on board."

"How can anyone say what a person does on his own time should be tied to the place he works," Mr. Ransom asks.

"People's perceptions are what they are," my father says. "Doesn't make it right; just makes it the way it is."

"Times sure have changed than when I was a kid," says Mr. Ransom. "How many accounts does a person have?"

"There are so many social media outlets. Facebook, Twitter, Instagram, LinkedIn, YouTube, Pinterest, Flick, and that's just some of the more popular ones. You don't have a Facebook account, Mr. Ransom?"

Matt's father lets out a bark of a laugh.

"I barely have email," he says. "In case you can't tell by looking at me, I'm not exactly the strip-down-the-computer-to-see-how-it-works kind of guy."

"You may not have one," I say. "But I bet Matthew does."

I log onto one of the social media sites that I'm on and search for Matthew's name. I find it and click on it.

"What's he have, Willy?" my father asks when he sees my reaction to what I've found. I look at him hoping he understands I'm unsure of what I should do.

"It's all right," he says. "Go on and tell Mr. Ransom. He's asked to know. So, let the man know."

I let out a sigh as I show Mr. Ransom the screen.

"Well, for starters, Matthew posts a lot of things that are…" I pause thinking of an appropriate word. "…Risqué."

Matthew's primary social media page is littered with videos of bikini-clad women, parties, drinking, and posts that feature lots of swear words.

It's Mr. Ransom's turn to loudly sigh. He shakes his head, muttering loudly.

"I swear, that boy is going to drive me crazy…

"According to one survey provided by recruiters, social media is not the sole deciding factor of who gets hired. But if it's down between two candidates, most agree that social media will usually play an influential factor."

"I see now why Matthew keeps coming up short," Mr. Ransom says. "I'm embarrassed. I'm sorry you had to see that, Willy."

"Don't be, Justin," says my father. "Matthew is not alone here. Many people do not know how to use the Internet responsibly. Its greatest strength is how connected it makes everyone. Unfortunately, that's its biggest weakness as well."

"What a person posts and shares with the world reflects not only on a person's interests, but also his character," I say.

"This will all change tonight, I can assure you that," Mr. Ransom says. Judging from the seriousness in the tone of his voice, I think Matt is going to catch an earful. "Willy, what can I do to thank you?"

"If you could, I'd like you to do two favors for people."

Confused, Mr. Ransom looks at my father who smiles and laughs.

"People helping people. That's how clients reimburse my daughter's efforts," my father says.

"Clients? Is that what I am?"

"Cyber Oracle. At your service," I say, handing him a business card.

"Well, how about that," Mr. Ransom says.

"Crazy isn't it? My daughter's changing the world, one Internet user at a time."

Chapter Six

On Saturday, I go to Washington, D.C., with Josie, Betta, and Tamara. One of our favorite things to do is to walk the Mall and see the monuments. The Lincoln Memorial is one of my favorite monuments in a city full of them. Same with Tamara. Betta likes the Vietnam Veterans Memorial because her grandfather served in the military during that conflict.

We also like to eat lunch at the food trucks that park down a few blocks from the Mall. Sometimes there will be a line of five or six trucks with different types of food from places like Thailand or Bangladesh. There was even a Hawaiian fusion truck one week, whatever that is.

I grab a Korean rice bowl. Betta gets a pizza from a pizza truck. Betta is forever eating pizza, she just can't get enough. Tamara settles for a gooey mess of grilled cheese. Josie doesn't get anything to eat.

"I'm not hungry," she says. There's something in her voice that tells me something's not right. I want to ask her a few more questions, but my friends are already searching for a long bench near a small park where kids play.

"You sure you don't want a bite?" Betta asks, chewing through melted mozzarella. "This is so good." When it comes to Italian food, she's true to her roots.

"Ugh," Josie says, dismissing the question and looking at her cell phone. Sometimes I think she spends too much time on the phone.

"Who you texting now?" Tamara says, blowing on a spoonful of piping-hot rice.

"Nunya," Josie says.

"Who's that?"

"Nunya business," Josie says.

We all groan. Her jokes can be corny.

I look over at the playground and see these three kids about eight or nine running around crazily. They don't seem to be playing any game, at least that I can tell. They each hold cell phones in their hands.

"What's going on over there?" I ask to any of my friends who are listening.

Betta looks up.

"Who? Those kids by the swings?"

"No," Tamara says. "I think she's talking about the kids by the sandpit."

"No, nitwits," I say. "Them!"

I point to the two boys and one girl laughing and running around. They wave their cell phones in their hands.

"Oh, that," Betta says, licking her fingers then cleaning them with a napkin. "Here, let me show you."

Betta removes her cell phone from her pocket.

"It's a new game," she says. "You play it on your phone. It's kind of fun."

"Oh, no," says Tamara. "Not you too, Betta. We've already lost one friend to her cell phone. Now you?"

"I don't play it all the time," Betta says. "Just when there's no one around. I'm telling you, it's kind of cool."

"Show me," I say. I must admit I'm kind of curious as to what game that's played on the phone has snared the attention of the one girl who uses her cell phone less than me. Betta gets up and inserts herself in between Josie and me.

"Slipper Ghosts," she says. "It really is fun! You use the smart phone to see where the ghosts are, and you try to capture them. The cool thing is that it combines the real world with the game. Look!"

Betta shows me her cell phone screen. Sure enough, even though I'm seeing the tree through the phone's camera, the game's software transposed a Slippery Ghost – this one Rocking Red – over the scene so it made the red specter look like it was standing in front of the tree.

"That is pretty cool," I admit. I'm not big into gaming, but even I am impressed when technology does something like this.

"The object of the game is to collect as many ghosts as you can, develop some of the ones you want to keep, and do battle with other ghost trainers. That's what they call people who play Slippery Ghosts."

"Oh yeah," Tamara says. "Everyone is playing that game. My cousin Marcus in New York was telling me that the police had to put out warnings to drivers to keep an eye out for careless ghost trainers stumbling into the streets and bumping into things like telephone poles and mail boxes."

"That's crazy," I say. "And dangerous."

"Don't worry about me, Web," Betta says. "I'm careful. But the faster you get the ghost the faster you get to the higher levels."

Blue light flickers on Betta's screen.

"Blue Ice Devil!" she squeals. "Be right back."

With that, Betta leaps to her feet and runs into the playground.

"Would you look at that girl?" Tamara says. "Makes me think it's be better if she just texted like Josie."

"What?" Josie says. She's still focused on her phone. Her thumbs poke rapidly on the letter screen.

"Can you just put it down for one second?" I say.

"You're not my mom," Josie says. She gets up and storms away.

Tamara gives me a look and shrugs her shoulders.

"Do you know what's going on with her?" I ask.

"Beats me," she says. "That girl is juggling so many boys she should get a part time job at a circus."

I sigh. I don't know if I'm as worried about Josie as I am wondering why I haven't been bitten by the boy-bug yet. I dig my Tablet out of my bookbag with another smaller device.

"You launching a satellite, Web?" Tamara asks, as she watches me boot up my laptop.

"I just want to check out this Slippery Ghost game. I'm curious about something."

"Yeah, but what's that thing?" She points to the small box.

"It's a wireless router that acts as a mobile Wi-Fi hotspot," I tell her. "I turn this on and log onto the Internet just like any other Wi-Fi network."

"Boy, you are so smart, I think you forget the easy things. Like, hello? The park has free Wi-Fi." She points to a sign that says that very thing.

"Free Wi-Fi is not the same as good Wi-Fi. Or secure. It's an open network. Yes, it will get you on the Internet but anyone with a little know-how and curiosity can see what you're looking at."

"Give it a rest, Web," Tamara says. "It's not like you're doing Wall Street trading. What do you need to be secure for?"

I give T one of my, "Are you kidding me?" looks. She may be one of my best friends, but I swear, it's like she learns nothing from me. I see why my father always says nothing surprises him when it comes to people's perceptions about technology. So many people don't consider how they get on the Internet and what can happen to their devices once they do.

I pull up a few articles on Slippery Ghosts. It was really a silly game, but I can see how people get hooked on it. Bright cool graphics and an interactive platform are usually an unbeatable selling point for the gaming enthusiasts.

"Oh, man!"

I look up and see Betta looking at her phone. She shakes it and fidgets with the buttons. She's obviously exasperated about something.

"What's the matter, Betta?" I ask. "Did those Slippery Ghosts get past you?"

"No," she says glumly. She walks back to the bench and cops a squat. "Something's wrong with my dumb phone. I told my dad I need the new one, but he just laughed. This is no laughing matter. I'm about to enter the Third Dimension. I need my phone to work."

I try to conceal a smile. I can imagine Betta putting forth an argument to her attorney-father, selling him on the need to pay for the latest model phone so she could conquer a game, that in all likelihood, is going to be outdated in a month.

"Can I see it? Maybe I can tweak it a bit," I offer her.

Betta's eyes brighten.

"If you could do that, I'd be your best friend," she says.

"You are one of my best friends," I remind her.

"Yeah, but I'd be like, a super best friend."

"Lucky me," I tease her. "Okay, hand it over. Let's see if the Oracle can come through."

Betta hands me her phone. The face has a crack and there are dings and nicks on the plastic holder. If you looked up "clumsy" in the dictionary, you'd see her picture alongside the definition, which is a shock given how graceful she moves on the soccer field.

"You ought to clean this thing occasionally," I tell her. I wipe some sticky thing off my hand.

"Sorry," she says.

I check out the phone's main page and scan through the Apps. She has a ton of Apps on her phone, it's amazing she can even use it to make a call. I power off the phone, wait a few seconds, then turn it on. That's a cell phone's way of rebooting.

"Did you drop it?" I ask her as the phone warms up.

"No," she says. "Well, not like in the last ten minutes. I did last night but it landed on the carpet."

"You should get one of those thick rubber guards," I tell her.

"I have one," she says, her voice chipper.

"Just not on the phone," I say.

"I keep forgetting," she says.

When the phone reboots, I begin to scroll through it. I try to access some Apps and the phone still isn't working quite right. The app icons look blurry, and the touch screen seems to have lost its sensitivity, even after I clean it thoroughly.

I bite my lip thoughtfully as I work through the various scenarios in my head.

"Let me ask you something, Betta," I say. "When did you download the Slipper Ghosts App?"

"Originally? Had to be a month or two ago. But the phone was working fine then."

"Have there been any updates?"

Betta gives me a look like I'm crazy.

"I may not be a techie, but even I know that games always have updates. I downloaded the recent version last night."

My face must have changed because a worried look crossed over hers.

"You think its infected with a virus?"

"That's possible. Either that or the App has some bugs in it. Did you download it from the main app store?"

"I don't know. Maybe? To be honest, I just went to the first site I saw that had the new version."

I nod my head the way my father does when he thinks he's solved an issue.

"Come on, Web," Betta pleads. "Is it doomed or what?"

"Infected? Yeah. Doomed? That needs to be determined. You see, Betta, part of the problem is where you downloaded the site. You should never go to any untrusted site and download software to any device, whether it's a smartphone, laptop, PC, or Tablet. You just never know what you're getting. Did you know that even respected App stores have been known to offer Apps that have bugs or viruses in them?"

"You're right, Web. I know better than that."

"Apps can be great fun, but you have to be careful about them, even the ones that don't have malware in them. Once downloaded onto your device, some Apps can access all your most personal and protected information and send it onto untrusted and harmful destinations."

"Really? Like what?"

"Anything on your smartphone. Internet search history, chats, photos, documents, your location... This is the type of information that you don't want to get out to just anybody, especially the bad guys. Once they get this type of info, there are several tricky things that they can do to steal your identity. Or worse, they can pretend to be you and target someone else."

"People really do that?"

"You bet they do. Did you know that on some smartphones, some of these apps can access more than 124 different permissions? That includes turning your camera on and even recording your conversations. That's spy stuff."

"That is very scary," Betta says.

"Let this be a lesson for you in the future regarding what you put on your phone and what you allow it access to. Always make sure that any default setting is disabled and configured the way you want it to be. Sometimes manufacturers leave it up to the individual to change them to suit preferences. Otherwise, they let them be open and accessible."

"Thanks, I will," Betta says. She sighs and looks at me. "But do you think you can fix it?"

I study the phone for a little bit. This is new territory for me, but even though I'm not a phone aficionado, it is still just a computer at its core. I pull up a search engine and find some computer security sites. I start looking for articles on cell phone apps, bugs, and look to see if I can find any known problems with the Slippery Ghosts game. After reading a few articles and blogs on cell phone security, I look up to see Betta staring intently on me.

"Well? Can you fix it, Web?"

I can't resist teasing my friend. My face gets serious and I exhale loudly.

"Betta," I say. "I don't know how to tell you this... Your phone... well..."

She leans in close to me, hanging on to every word.

"...I can fix it."

It takes a moment for the news to register on my friend's face. When she realizes what I've said, she slaps my arm.

"What are you trying to do, give me a heart attack?" she exclaims. She feigns anger, but I can tell that she's very relieved.

Emilio Iasiello

"First thing we're going to do is switch the phone into Airplane Mode. That will stop the transmission of any data that may be happening now."

I hand back her phone and show her how to switch to Airplane Mode.

"Next," I continue, "is we have to remove the App. Go under "Settings" and find "Applications." Then search for the app. Tap it and then tap "uninstall.""

"That's seems easy enough," Betta says. "But what if it doesn't budge?"

"Great question," I say, impressed with Betta's curiosity. "If that happens, the first thing you should do is boot into 'Safe Mode' to disable all third-party apps. This varies on the device, but essentially you just bring up the power menu and long-press the 'power off' entry. Then you'll be prompted to boot into 'Safe Mode.' Once booted, go to your 'Main Settings' menu, select 'Applications,' and find the bad app in the 'Downloaded' section and delete it."

I observe Betta as she successfully finds and deletes the bad application.

"I did it." Betta looks at me, surprises she was able to solve a computer problem, with just a little direction. "Did you see that? I did it."

"Good job, Betts," I say. "There's so much unnecessary fear when it comes to troubleshooting technology. People would actually shock themselves if they knew that they could actually fix many of the problems that they face daily."

"Maybe I'll get a nickname like yours," she says. Now, I know she's teasing me.

"Sure, we'll call you User Error," I tell her.

"Seriously, thank you for your help."

"What are friends for? Just remember. While mobile Apps can be a lot of fun, you have to be careful where you download them from. Even from a respected App store can't guarantee every app to be without viruses or bugs. Did you know that a bunch of phony game Apps for children, from trusted mobile app stores, have been found to steal information from mobile devices?"

"I didn't know that," Betta says. "I'll be more careful next time I can assure you that. I don't need to go through this again."

"That's why we need to make sure that we are doing everything we can to educate ourselves about technology, so it continues to be helpful and not hurtful. But, now you have to do something for me."

"Name it."

"I fixed your phone. Next time someone needs some help, you pass the favor forward."

"Why not just email it forward?" Betta says, laughing.

"Ha-ha."

"I hear you, Web. And you got it. Now that's settled, shall we get the rest of the crew? They seem to have snuck away when the computer talk started."

She's right. I look around. I spot Tamara on the swings. Even though we're older we all still like parks. Swinging is one thing you never tire of. Even at school, Tamara will jump on a swing if one is available.

"Are you done playing around?" I yell at her. She sticks her tongue out at me.

"I was going to ask you the same thing," she yells back.

Betta and I walk over to her. The swing creaks loudly as Tamara pumps her legs back and forth.

"Where's the fourth Musketeer?" Betta asks.

We look around the park and find Josie sitting on a bench on the far end of the park. She is staring down at the phone in her hands. Her expression is blank, like she's thinking of something else.

"Hey, Josie! Josie!"

It takes all of us to yell her name before she looks up.

"What?"

"Um, we've been trying to get your attention for like five minutes," Tamara says.

"Sorry, my mind was somewhere else."

"Anyplace cool, like India?" Betta jokes.

Josie just looks at Betta without saying anything.

"I was just kidding," Betta says when she sees that the joke didn't hit its mark.

"Come on," I say. "Let's hit the Spy Museum."

"I'm sorry, guys. I'm not feeling so well right now."

"What's the matter?" I ask her.

"Nothing serious. I just need to go. I'll talk to you guys later."

With that, Josie walks away, headed to the Metro station.

"What's wrong with her?" Betta asks.

"I don't know," I say. "But I don't think it's because she's sick."

"I think it's that boy," Tamara says.

"She's seeing too much of him," Betta says.

"Actually, just the opposite. She told me yesterday that she hadn't seen him. That he was being cold to her."

"I can't say I didn't expect this," I say. "But I don't like to see any of my friends hurt."

I hope Josie is okay, but something tells me the problem lurks below the surface and not in the form of a viral bug.

The Spy Museum is the coolest museum in Washington, D.C. This is not to say that the other ones are not good too. Washington has the best museums in the world and most of them are free. When we hosted an exchange student from France last year, she was amazed that we didn't have to pay to see fine art or ancient artifacts.

This is the only museum in the entire country that is solely focused on to the shady world of espionage. There are so many exhibits that feature the actual devices of old time spy operations. The three of us drift through each exhibit, reading the behind-the-scenes stories of historic events, and gawking over the artifacts that were used to make these missions successful.

"How about that?" Tamara asks. "All of this and not one computer."

"She's got you there," Betta says.

"They didn't have them back then," I say, heading over to the next exhibit. "Spies use them now, you know."

"How can you spy with a computer?" Tamara asks.

"Are you kidding? How do you not? Look, the Internet connects the world together. Governments, companies, schools, militaries, everything. Spies use special tools and exploit vulnerabilities just like any other cyber criminal. Only instead of stealing money, they steal other things like information and plans, things like that."

"She's right, girls."

We turn to see an older man dressed in sports jacket and slacks. He has perfectly short white hair and a well-groomed moustache.

"Sorry to interrupt. I'm Pete Mathers, one of the curators here."

"Spies really use computers? No lie?" Tamara asks.

"No lie. Do you know what makes a good spy? The ability to get information without getting caught. At the very heart of it, that's what spies do. The movies exaggerate and glamorize spy craft and spy missions. In the end, we want information. And we don't want to get caught."

"We? Like you are a spy?" Betta asks. Her eyes get big like they do when she's very interested in something.

"Well, I was. A long time ago. Now I just bring the old missions to light for the public. Things that have been overlooked or unknown until now."

"Cool."

"It can be. But to be honest, a lot of spy work is making connections and figuring out ways to get information. As your friend has astutely pointed out, the Internet has facilitated information gathering. Same thing we did back in the Cold War but just digitally instead of manually."

"So, there are no more actual spies?" Betta asks. It's a good question and I acknowledge this by giving her a nod.

"There were always be real people spies," Mr. Mathers says. "Computers and cyberspace are just two more tools for them to use. People are careless about what they leave on their computers."

"And securing them," I add.

"Exactly. For a spy, any information obtained can be valuable. Even bits of information that don't seem important."

"You'd be surprised how many people have files that have their personal information and passwords," I say.

"And compromising data like letters or photos. These can be used to blackmail a target and coerce them into doing things they don't want to do."

"That's horrible," Betta says.

"It is. But it's a part of espionage. You get those people to spy for you. But that brings up a whole other type of spy – the one who catches the people that are spying."

"How do you catch a spy?" Tamara asks.

118

"The first thing is behavior. This is usually the first thing that will give you a heads up if something is off. Are they acting differently? Eating more than usual, eating less? Are they drinking alcohol or drugs to compensate? Are they crying more, avoiding people? These are what we call indicators. They don't necessarily guarantee something's wrong, but they are a sign that something could be."

I pause. I can't help but think of Josie's behavior lately. She's been distant from us and I can't remember the last time I saw her eat at lunch.

"Someone's mind is working," Mr. Mathers says. "Think any harder and there will be smoke coming out of your ears."

"You've just given me an idea, Mr. Mathers," I tell him.

"Then I've done my job," he says. "I hope you enjoy the museum, and if I can answer any question, do not hesitate to ask."

The ride home on the Metro keeps me deep in thought. Tamara and Betta chatter away noisily about spies but I'm focused on Josie. I don't think she's a spy or anything but her unusual behavior has got me thinking. First there's that boy. Then she spends most of her free time at the mall with him. And now suddenly she's not herself. The bubbly, boy-crazy girl who loves to laugh has been replaced with someone whose somber, sad, and irritable.

The connection is there somewhere.

I must figure out where that is.

Chapter Seven

Saturday is Betta's birthday party. Everyone is there except for Josie, who is sick. Betta's parents are fun people – you can tell they like to have a good time even at a kid's party. Everything is decorated – bright colors, neon, and bold designs. There are face painters, a magician, tons of games and prizes. And the food – there are pizzas, cakes, cupcakes, chicken fingers, chips, dips, and even cut-up vegetables, if that's your thing.

But the party doesn't end when everyone leaves with their party bags. Tamara and I are staying for a sleep over. Like I said, Betta's parents are cool.

The day was a blast. I got five tattoos and came in second in the three-legged race. Tamara broke the emoji piñata and instead of candy (even the Ianellis had a limit as to how much sugar they were going to feed hyper kids), it was filled with small knick-knack toys.

Later that afternoon, after everyone left, Betta, Tamara, and I sit on the back porch.

"This was the best party, Betta," Tamara says. "You set the bar high for the rest of us. You hear that Web? You're up next."

Even though my birthday is in two months, I'd be lying to say that I haven't thought about what I wanted at least a million times. I'm leaning toward a computer theme (surprise, surprise) and maybe make the whole party centered around solving a case. I haven't asked my dad yet, but I think he'd be on board with that. Not sure how the kids would like it though.

"Anyone hungry?" Betta's dad asks, poking his head out the backdoor. "There's still some pizza left."

Tamara and Betta groan. They are stuffed.

"No thanks, Mr. I," I say. "If I eat anything more, pizza will be coming out of my ears!"

"Ok, if you need anything, just holler. We'll be in the living room watching TV."

"Come on, Web," Tamara presses. "I know you have to be thinking about your party. Thinking is kind of your thing."

"Okay," I confess. "I was thinking a mystery theme. We have to solve a case Only, you know, using computers."

"Sounds cool," Betta says.

"Sounds geeky," Tamara says. She flashes me a grin. "Kidding, Web."

"Ha-ha," I say. "I think it can be interesting. Let me show you what I had in mind. Betts, can I borrow your computer?"

"Sure," it's in my room. "Let's go."

Betta's bedroom is decorated wall-to-wall posters of everything ranging from boy bands to horses. Lots of horses.

Betta leads us to her desk. She boots up the laptop.

"So, I was thinking there was a robbery. Some cyber thieves broke in and stole some money. Our job will be to find out who it is. If we do it right, each clue will lead to another clue that will reveal the identity of criminal."

"Oh, you know what would be cool?" Betta says. "That one of us is the criminal."

"I like where you're going with that," Tamara says. "I'd be great on the sly."

I roll my eyes. Tamara doesn't realize that she must be adept at using computers if she thinks she can be a sly cyber operator.

Suddenly, there's a bing. I look at the screen. An Instant Message pops up. It says, "How's the birthday girl?"

The screen name says: "NatsFan"

I make a face. This is odd.

"Who's this?" I ask Betta. She looks over at the screen. She smiles and answers the IM.

"Some kid I met online at District Down-Low," she says. District Down-Low is a site that most school kids go on to vent, bully people, and act childish. Some kids at school think it's funny to read some of the strings but I find them abusive and repulsive.

"Why are you going there?" Tamara asks. Last year some kids at school made up a rumor about Tamara being adopted and spread it on District Down-Low.

"I don't know," Betta says. "Curiosity mostly. Some things are funny."

"I don't think so," Tamara says icily. "You know what happened to me."

"I don't read any of those posts. I just usually sit in one of the chatrooms and just read the stuff people type. He found me there and hit me up. I didn't answer him the first few times he pinged me, but finally I said, what the heck? It's just talking."

"Who is it?" I ask. "Do you know his name?"

"He goes to school in the next town. Gary something-or-other. He's thirteen and plays baseball for Yorktown middle school."

"How do you know that if you don't know him?" Tamara asks.

"It's what he told me." Tamara gives her a look. "Okay, I don't know-know," Betta concedes.

"Betta, you shouldn't talk to people online you don't know," Tamara says. "Even I know that."

"But this is your IM," I say, leaning in close to the screen. "Doesn't Down-Low have a chat program attached to the site?"

"It does," Betta says. "After we talked a bit on the Down-Low he asked me to go private."

A metaphoric red flag pops up before my eyes.

"He moved you quickly from an online community to private conversations," I muse aloud. Oh yeah, "Gary" is a slick operator all right. "What else did he ask you? Think carefully."

Betta pauses to think for a moment. I can tell she's really racking her brain.

"Hobbies, my favorite subjects at school," Betta says.

The hairs on the back of my neck immediately spring on end.

"Wait – you told him what school you go to?" I ask.

"Sure, so what? Lots of kids go to that school."

I bit my lip as I worked through this new development.

"Anything else?"

A dark look crosses Betta's face.

"He asked me where our computer was at home. I thought that strange."

A second red flag pops up in front of my eyes.

"Betta? How did he know it was your birthday?"

"I'm not sure," Betta admits.

"This is the problem. He seems to know a lot about you, but you don't really know a lot about him."

Betta frowns. I think I was finally making sense to her.

"He knows where I go to school and my birthday."

"Have you told him your name?" I ask.

"No. I don't think so."

"Well, he's got a head start in finding that out if he isn't who he says he is," I say.

"Do you really think Gary's like that?"

"I don't know anything about Gary. And neither do you. The best-case scenario is that he's a kid over at Yorktown. The worst case is something far more serious. You must be careful about the information you provide online to people you don't know. There are a lot of dangerous people out there. There are a lot of predators."

"Right!" says Tamara. "Like that show where the reporter confronts those guys going to that young girl's house."

"Exactly."

As we sit there, "Gary" sends another IM. This time there is an attachment. I study the IM wondering what it could be.

"Are you going to open it?" Beta asks.

"No. There are so many things that can be wrong with it. It could be an inappropriate picture, or even have a virus attached to it. Sometimes people send malware that once it infects your computer gives them complete control of it."

"How is that possible?" Tamara asks.

"The malware takes advantage of a computer's weaknesses. Once that happens, the sender can do anything – listen to the computer's microphone and hear us talking, steal any photos or information that's stored on the computer, even turn on your webcam and spy on you!"

"I heard about that! Someone did that to the girl that won the Miss Teen competition last year. He recorded her while she was changing and spread it on the Internet."

"What should I do, Web?" she asks. Her voice is tinged with fear and rightfully so.

"One, stop chatting to him. Two, get off that site. It's nothing but trouble."

"Time to go, Gary-boy," Betta says.

She clicks him off.

"Good girl," I say. "You need to chat with anyone, that's what we're here for."

"She's right," Tamara says. "Besides, you can't get any better cyber friend than this girl right here."

She rubs my head with her hand like I was a puppy dog.

"One more thing," I say taking over control of the keyboard. "Time to make sure you're running a clean machine."

I go to the antivirus program and make sure it's up to date. Then I run a full scan on the computer for known threats.

"Just to make sure that nothing bad has gotten into the computer," I say.

"This was a close call. I should have known that something was up when he asked about the computer."

"He was asking because he wanted to know if it was in a place where your parents were around," I say.

"That's awful!" Tamara says.

"I feel like a jerk," Betta says.

"Don't be. We don't know if this is a predator or not. That's one of the biggest dangers of talking with people on the Internet – you don't really know who people are. They can pass themselves off as anyone. Now there are millions of people that use the Internet and they're not all predators. But that's why we have to make sure we protect ourselves at all times."

The computer scan finishes. Fortunately, Betta doesn't have a lot of files or else this could take a long time. The more stuff on your computer, the longer scans take. Of course, you can be selective about what you scan, like say, a hard drive, or a removable media device. You can even run scans just to search for rootkits. But putting your mind at ease requires you to be sure, and that requires running a full scan.

Anyway, no threats are detected so Betta can feel a bit better.

Thirty seconds later, an Instant Message pops up on screen from Gary. "Where are youuuuuu?????" it says.

The same message repeats itself three more times.

"He doesn't like being shut out," Tamara says.

"He doesn't seem so nice now," Betta says, as the IM content becomes more insistent and mean.

"Time to cool off, Gary," Betta says. Then she goes to her profile on chat messenger and deletes her account. She turns off the computer.

"Tomorrow, we will delete this account, and set up a gender-neutral one instead. Also, keep records of everything Gary said to you in case he turns out to be something other than an immature boy."

"Thanks, Web."

"That's what friends are for. And I have two of the best ones right here!"

We give each other a group hug.

When we break our embrace, Betta's face brightens.

"Who could go for another piece of cake?"

At bedtime, we sleep on the floor in Betta's room. Each of us has a sleeping bag. The lights are off but we each have a flashlight. When its someone's turn to speak, she places the flashlight under her chin, so it spookily lights up her face.

Ghost stories never get old, and no matter how much we try to convince ourselves that we aren't afraid of anything, a good story will always make us tuck our head under a blanket or pillow.

Betta finishes a story about campers in Maine and something called The Green Slime." She's a good storyteller and knows how to keep listeners hanging on every word. When she's finished, we all seem to tighten our circle a little more.

"I wish Josie was here," Betta says. "I hope she's feeling better."

"I'm not so sure she's sick," I say. "There's something wrong but I don't think it has to do with an upset stomach or fever."

"True that," Tamara says directly. "It's that boy. Whatever is happening, he's connected to it somehow. I just know it."

"I think you're right," I say. "Thing is, I'm not sure how."

"Maybe we should follow him?" Betta says.

"We don't even know where he lives," Tamara says, rolling her eyes. She tosses a pillow at Betta.

"No," I say. "We need to ask her. We're her friends. She knows us. She trusts us."

The others fall asleep. I stare up at the ceiling. Betta's room is so cool. She has these glow-in-the-dark stars fastened to the ceiling. Her dad is an astronomy nut and has laid them out to reflect a winter time constellation pattern. Orion, Gemini, Canes Major. In the spring, he will change them out to reflect the new season's patterns.

My thoughts drift to Josie. I know she's in trouble. I can feel it.

I just hope she's not in too deep.

Or we're not too late.

Chapter Eight

I walk into my house the next morning to find my father and mother sitting at the kitchen table. Their faces are grim, so I know it's a serious conversation.

My mother turns toward me when she hears the front door close.

"Sweetie," she says. "You nearly gave me a heart attack."

"Sorry," I say. "What's going on? Did something happen?"

My parents share a look. I know whatever it is, it must be serious. That's an adult look, all eye contact and no words spoken.

"Sit down, Willy," my father says.

I get a queasy feeling in my stomach. I wonder if I'm in trouble although I haven't done anything wrong that I can remember. I sit across from my parents. For a few moments, no one says anything.

"Mom? Dad? You're scaring me."

"I'm afraid I'm terrified," my mother says. "I'm sick to my stomach."

"When is the last time you talked to your friend Josie?"

"Josie? Why?"

"Please answer the question, honey," my mom says. "This is important."

"I don't know. I didn't see her at school and she didn't come to Betta's birthday party. Is she okay?"

"Health-wise? She's fine, thank God," my mother says. "She got into a little trouble is all."

"What kind of trouble?"

My mom looks at my father. He leans in close, putting his elbows on the table.

"I'm going to ask you a question," he says. "I need you to be completely honest with me. Okay? Can you do that for me?"

"Of course," I say. "You can ask me anything. You know that."

"What do you know about sexting?"

I freeze in my seat. Sexting is a thing that's been going around school for a while. People talk about it, but usually it's just that – talk. I've heard of high schoolers sending dirty pictures to each other, but I've never seen anything like that.

"Just what you know. Kids are doing it. I'm not. I swear."

My father gives me a half-smile.

"I know that, Willy," he says. "Believe me, I know. This is not about you."

A small swell of relief comes out of my mouth. But it's soon replaced by a new fear.

"Josie?" I ask.

My parents share another look. My mom takes the lead in responding.

"There was an incident," she says. "Josie's involved. We're not sure how deep the problem is. Her parents reached out to us and got your dad involved."

"Is she okay?"

"She's shook up, honey. Pretty badly."

"Can I see her?"

"I'll talk to her father," my dad says.

Dinner is a quiet time. The music of forks and knives. I can hear my father in the other room on the phone. His voice is deep and mellow. I can tell he has his thinking cap on and he is listening more than he's talking, getting the facts and putting them into order in his head.

He hangs up the phone and enters the room.

"Why don't you stop by and see her after school tomorrow," he says. "The teachers have collected her schoolwork and you can bring it to her."

"Ok," I say.

Then my father comes over to me and gives me a big bear hug.

I hug him back. When we finally break the hug, I can see tears in his eyes.

"What's wrong, Dad?"

"I'm just thankful," he says.

"Thankful for what?"

"For you," he says.

My mom puts her hand on my hand and gives it a squeeze. Sometimes you forget that your parents are not these omnipotent people that can basically do anything. You forget that they can cry like you do and get hurt like you can.

"I love you, Willy."

"I love you too, Dad."

The next day at school, I find out that both Betta and Tamara are sick, leaving me solo for key social activities like lunch and recess. During the first recess period, I walk around the playground. The alone-time lets me think what I'm going to say to Josie when I see her. I know she's torn up over this, and rightfully so. I am so mad at this kid I want to tear his face off for hurting my friend.

The whispered talks of a group of girls by the gymnasium breaks me from my thoughts. Kim, a pretty girl with short black hair and perfect white teeth, is in the center of three other girls. They are all a grade ahead of me.

"Don't kid yourself," Kim says. "Everyone does it."

"I don't think so," says another girl I know as Cathy. "I wouldn't do it."

"You're like six months younger than me," Kim says. "Don't worry. You'll mature."

I must have been closer than I thought because when Kim sees me, she points.

"Even her friend did it," she says. "Isn't that right, Weeb?"

"Web," I say, correcting her. "And I don't know what you're talking about."

"Yah, right," she says. "That girl is your friend. The one that sexted that boy at Woodlawn. What's her name?"

"How do you know that?" I ask her.

"Hello? Do you know who I am? I got friends in every school in the county. If it happens, believe me, I know about it."

"Is that true?" a girl in a ponytail asks me.

"I don't know the facts yet," I say.

"Why would anyone want to do that?" asks another girl whose name I think is Nikki.

Kim shrugs her shoulders.

"Why does anyone do anything, stupid? It's fun," she says. "You send a pic to your boyfriend or a boy you're interested in. He sends you one back.

Don't be such a goody two-shoes. It's just a new type of flirting."

"That's not flirting," I say. "Your body is private and should be treated as such. Once you send a picture out in cyberspace it's there forever. You can't get it back and you have no control over what someone does with it."

"I thought you are supposed to be the computer geek," Kim says. "If you use that program that automatically deletes the photo in ten seconds, then it's pretty much harmless."

I shake my head. So many people think that computer technology can be 100 percent secure and that's just not the case. As my father always says, steer clear of any company that makes a device or a program and guarantee complete privacy.

"That's not true," I say. "Look, the program may delete the photo from the phone, but the digital data is still on a server somewhere."

"Yeah? Where is it?"

"I don't know," I say. "But for someone who sent a racy picture? You don't either. That's the scary part. You can't delete cyberspace. Oh, and for your information, there's a lot someone can do in the seconds it takes for that photo to disappear from a phone. "

"Really?" Kim asks. "Like what?"

Although the attitude is still in her voice, it's noticeably less apparent.

"They can take a screenshot or save it to another app on the phone," I say. "Once they have that they can send it to anyone."

"That's what happened to Jessica Carbone," says the ponytail-haired girl. "She was dating that guy Vikas. When she broke up with him last year he put it on one of those sites, so everyone could see."

"I heard a bunch of boys talking about some website that has photos like that," Cathy says. "There are even pictures of boys on it too."

"Not all boys do that," Kim protests. It's evident from her body language that she is getting very uncomfortable and not so sure of herself.

"No, of course not, but you can't guarantee that," I say. "I think Jessica Carbone will attest to that. And depending on what happened to my friend, so will she."

"And even if they don't post it somewhere online, they certainly can show it to their friends," Cathy says. "Do you want to be passed around like that?"

Kim suddenly becomes quiet.

"Well, no, not exactly…" she says.

"And did you know that sexting, or whatever you want to call it, can be very hurtful to people? Girls get harassed because their pictures are sent to their classmates, friends, family. Even if you change schools that type of reputation can follow you. Some girls have even taken their lives because they couldn't handle the bullying that they received because they thought their 'sexts' were protected, and they weren't."

Silence settles in the small group. The talk had been eye opening for the girls. Their faces show concern and worry.

"So, if you ask me, it's not harmless at all," I say to Kim. "I would hope my boyfriend would never ask me for one, and I certainly hope any boy I'm interested in would never even consider asking me to send him one. It's not just disrespectful, it's dangerous."

"I know that now," Kim says. "It's so hard to talk about this stuff with my parents."

"Give them a chance. They're not as old as we sometimes think. But talking with friends is always good too. Besides, we girls got to stick together," I say.

I'm about to leave when Kim calls out.

"Hey, Web? Thanks."

"You're welcome."

"I hope your friend's okay."

"Me too."

In the afternoon, I get off the bus near Josie's house. I carry an armful of books to her front door and ring the doorbell. I've rehearsed what I'm going to say to my friend, but I've forgotten everything by the time the door answers. Josie's mom lets me in.

"How are you, Willy?" she asks me as I enter.

"Good, Mrs. G." Josie's last name is Gladstone.

"Thank you for bringing Josie this," she says. "She's not up to return to school just yet."

"It's completely understandable," I say. "Can I bring these up to her?"

A half-smile from Mrs. Gladstone.

"I think she'd like that," she says. "She misses her friends."

"We miss her," I say.

"Go up and see her."

At the top of the stairs I head to the door at the end of the hall. It has a poster of a double rainbow on it. I gently knock.

"Josie? It's me, Web."

There is a long silent pause. I hear Josie getting off her bed and walking toward the door. She unlocks the door."

I open it and find Josie back on her bed. She curls up in a tight ball with her back toward me. I walk over to her desk and set the books and notebooks on it.

"Here's your classwork." I'm not sure what to say. "How are you feeling?"

"How do you think?"

"I'm sorry, Josie."

"You're sorry, I'm sorry, everyone's sorry," she laments. I can hear her fight back the sobs.

I go over to her and sit down on the bed.

"It's horrible, I know," I say. "If there's one positive, it's that it was caught in time. I heard my father talking about it with the police. That boy's going to be expelled from school."

"He deserves worse," she says.

"He does. You're right. People need to respect people a lot more. Everyone is someone's son or daughter. That's something that needs to be protected, not exploited."

"Yeah."

"But there's something else that we can do, I think, that needs to be done."

"What's that?"

"We can respect ourselves. We start by understanding that what we have is what makes us unique. Our bodies, our feelings, are not to be shared so carelessly. They're special. And the people that want to be a part of that must take that seriously. But we can't expect them to do that if we don't do it ourselves first."

Josie looks up at me.

"I messed up," she says.

"No," I say. "You made a mistake. And mistakes can be rectified."

"What can I do?"

And now the tears start. I reach out and hold my friend tightly as she sobs. Her tears are hot and wet against my neck.

"You're a kid. You did a kid thing. Just make sure you don't repeat the mistake."

"I don't know if I can go back to school," she says. "I don't know if I can handle all of the stares, all of the talk."

"Sure, you can," I tell her. "You're not alone. You have me, T, Betta. And you have a few others too you probably don't even realize."

"Really? Like who?"

"All of those girls that might be thinking about doing what you did but didn't because your story convinced them not to."

"You think so?"

"I know so. Kids like us must know that just because something is popular doesn't make it good. And just because people are doing something we don't agree with doesn't make it right."

Finally, Josie breaks a smile.

"Thanks, Web," she says.

"You're my friend, Josie. You will always be my friend."

Josie hugs me so tightly I don't think she'll ever let go.

And part of me doesn't want her to.

That night at dinner, Mom serves me my favorite, spaghetti and meatballs with garlic bread and a cold salad with zesty lemon dressing. After we say Grace, Dad starts making our plates.

"How did it go today with Josie," my mom asks, passing me a plate.

"She's distraught," I say. "But I think I helped her feel better."

"I'm sure you did."

"The boy has been questioned by the police. Fortunately, this appears to be an isolated incident. But I have no doubt that if he hadn't been stopped, he probably would have done this to other girls."

"Is he going to jail?" I ask.

"Probably not. But if he was a couple of years older, he'd be arrested and convicted of traffic in child pornography."

A chill shot up and down my spine.

"Sexting is no joke," he says.

I finish chewing a forkful of spaghetti.

"I told that to a bunch of girls today at recess," I say. "The incident with Josie came up. So, did Jessica Carbone."

"Oh dear, Lord," says my mother. "I totally forgot about that poor girl."

"One of the girl's said she had sent a racy picture to a boy."

"Good grief," my father says, putting down his fork. "What's it take to get through to the youth of today?"

"It's different, Dad. Things are discussed more openly than they probably were when you were a kid."

"That's not entirely true," my mother says. "The times may be different, but the conversation is the same. What is different is that technology makes it easier for unscrupulous people to exploit others and invade their privacy."

"Amen to that, Letitia," my father says. "Who was it, Willy?"

I pause. Even though I have an open relationship with my parents, and will tell them most things, I don't immediately share the girls' names. My dad senses my apprehension immediately.

"Forget that," he says. "May I ask what you all talked about?"

"One girl said it wasn't a big deal what happened, and we had an open discussion about it. I was able to show them how sexting isn't cool, that it could lead to real problems down the line."

"She's wrong," my father says.

"I know. And I told her why."

"What did your friends say?" my mother asks.

"At first they didn't know what to make of it. Peer pressure is big, and I didn't want them to think that just because one person does it, that everyone should do it. We had an open talk and they agreed with me. The one didn't at first, but she came around. Explaining how it's impossible to erase pictures from the Internet was quite the lesson for them. Especially when I told them how some kids can't escape the attention."

I turn to my father.

"That's why I don't want to mention any names right now. I got her on the straight and narrow. If I think she's headed back in the wrong direction, I'll tell you then."

My father nods his head. He grabs my hand and squeezes.

I beam a smile. I hand my empty plate to my mom.

"Can I have some more pasta, Mom?"

"Well, don't get too full on pasta," my mother says. "Your father is making sundaes for dessert.

That night my father reads me two bedtime stories, something he hasn't done in a long time. I want to ask him why now, but don't. He has a quiet satisfaction in reading to me, and I can't help but think he misses me when I was a young kid afraid of shadows and spiders. After he finishes reading the second book, he sits next to me and pats my leg.

"Kids are growing up so fast," he says. "That's what we as parents need to take from what happened to Jessica and Josie."

"Some do better with their children than others," I say. "As long as the lines of communication are kept open, I think that's important."

"I didn't tell you this before," he says. "But you know what really disturbed me about the site where Jessica's photos were posted?"

"What's that?"

"It was all inclusive. Young people from every race, every religion, and both rich and poor alike were in those pictures. You know like I do that three out of four teens own a cell phone, and that 19 percent of teens have sent sexually suggestive images of themselves to others."

"So, what's the answer?"

"We all have an educational role to play. Parents, schools, police, and most of all, the kids themselves. And you Willy, are one step ahead of us."

"I come from good stock."

Chapter Nine

Friday is *Take Your Kid to Work Day*, so I get to go with my dad to his office. I like going there because it's full of computers and people doing interesting things. Being a computer forensics expert, my dad investigates computer technology for clues to help police locate and convict bad guys that operate on the Internet. It's cool that there are people like him out there.

Dad parks in the lot next to the building. The guard at the gate waves at me as we stop, and he checks my dad's badge.

"Well, well, well, this must be the Oracle," he says to me.

I look at my father who smiles and shrugs.

"Word gets out," he says.

"How's business?" the guard asks me. The nametag on his shirt reads "Stan."

"Busy," I say. "I think I need to hire."
"Don't look at me," he says. "Computers to me are big paper weights. But I'm sure you are going to find some capable people in your dad's office."

Dad's office building is not much to look at. If you ask him, he will be the first to tell you that many government buildings are not like you see on TV shows. His building is brown, dirty, and looks like a boxer that has taken one too many punches and is barely standing.

"Are you sure your building is safe?" I tease him.

"You're hysterical, Willy," my dad says putting his arm around my shoulder. "Let's go."

My dad's immediate office is a bullpen of desks and chairs and phones and computer screens. There are other kids of varying ages walking around, talking to the some of the officers, and being introduced to one another.

"This is cool," I say.

"Wait until you see where we do a lot of the work," he says.

Dad introduces me to a series of men and women who work with him. Depending on the individuals, there are as many as two or three screens on their desks.

"Everyone has a critical role in this process," my father tells me. "Jan handles imagining and media. She 'bags and tags' all the data that arrives and is the lead analyst to go out and collect data from desktops, laptops, and servers."

The Web Paige Chronicles

Jan is a woman about my father's age. She has short dark brown hair and brown eyes. She gives me a bright smile and waves. I smile and wave back.

"Now Timothy," my dad continues, "is the processor. Once data is collected it must be searched through. That's where he comes in. He uses a special tool with predefined search parameters to filter through the data to look for specific things."

Timothy is in his thirties, and he likes to wear his sunglasses on top of his shaved head.

You've heard of trying to find a needle in a haystack?" Timothy asks. I nod. "Well, I'm the person that looks for that needle."

"Over there," directs my father toward a young serious-faced Indian man with glasses. He is the only one wearing a button-down shirt and tie. "That's Hardik. He's our mobile phone guru. With everyone having different brands of mobile phones now-a-days, and all being able to access the Internet through them, mobile phones are very important in the forensics process. Hardik recovers data from smartphones."

Hardik gives me a slight bow and a curt nod. I reciprocate.

"So," I say, turning to my father. "If they do all that work exactly what is it that you do?"

151

"I have the most important responsibility of everyone," he says. "I learn from people a heck of a lot smarter than me."

Timothy stands up and walks over to us.

"Don't let him fool you, Web. I can call you Web, can't I?"

"Everyone does except for my parents," I say.

"Well, Web, your dad is the person we 'smart' people go to when we can't figure something out."

I beam. I like it when my father is complimented. He pushes aside the complement by rolling his eyes and make a guffawing sound.

"Join the club," I say. "That's pretty much my daily existence."

The team ran us through a *day in the life* of the group, - from the process of identifying malware, reverse engineering it, and demonstrating how they run a various set of tools - to image hard drives and the steps they go through to conduct and record their analysis. I must be honest, some of the stuff got technical even for me. Before we leave, my father passes out various SWAG to all the kids. SWAG is *stuff we all get*, which basically consists of hats, t-shirts, and plastic cups with the team's logo on them.

As we walk to the car, my cell phone dings. It's a message from a friend of mine, Susan Tanaka. The text is cryptic but knowing Susan, I think it's serious.

"Hey Dad," I say. "Can we stop by a friend of mine's house? It's on the way home."

"Sure," he says. "Who is it?"

"Susan Tanaka," I say.

"Is it serious?"

I show him the text.

"Let's get going."

On the way to Susan's house, my dad asks what I thought of his office.

"The people are interesting," he says. "They make the day go by quickly and the work fun."

"I have to say, I was surprised how complex everything is. I mean, it's computer technology – of course it's going to be complex. But there are so many people specializing in so many specific areas."

"That's why we have so many people doing what they do. Computers are complex systems. People tend not to think so because there are so many of them and you can buy a good laptop cheaply. But what makes them run is code. Millions and millions of lines of code."

"And sometimes they have bugs in them," I say.

"Right. There are so many millions of lines that software companies find newer ones and put out patches, so people can fix the security hole."

I shake my head.

"How does one person wrap her mind around it all?" I ask.

One doesn't," he says. "Cyber security is a team effort from the lowest rung on the latter to the person sitting in the catbird seat."

We pull up in front of Susan Tanaka's house. My father waits in the car while I run up and knock on the door. Mrs. Tanaka opens the door.

"Hey Mrs. T," I say. "Susan texted me and says she needs some help."

"I'm glad you're here, Web," Mrs. Tanaka says. "Something seems to be bothering her and she won't tell me what. The last two nights she hasn't been sleeping well, and she barely eats. I'm not sure if it's a boy issue or something worse."

I draw my eyebrows together. "That doesn't sound like Susan at all," I say. "I've seen her eat a whole medium pizza."

"You're her friend. I'd be appreciative of anything you can do."

"Of course," I tell her. "Susan's a friend, and I do anything for my friends."

I walk up the stairs to Susan's room. I knock on the door. When no one answers, I knock again and then open the door.

"Susan…?" I say.

Susan's room is painted in lavender and is a collage of her diverse interests – boy bands, NASA space ships, and Japanese art. I find my friend on the floor staring at her laptop.

"Hey, space cadet," I say in a louder tone. "Didn't you hear me knock?"

Susan doesn't look away from the laptop screen. Her face is puffy, and there are wet streaks down her cheeks like she has been crying.

"What's the matter, Susan?" I ask.

"Nothing," Susan mumbles.

I walk over to her and looked at the screen. Susan is on the "District Down-Low." I groan when I recognize the sleazy site. Why this site is still allowed to be accessible is beyond me. It is a detriment to kids, of fake news and gossip, an enabler of insults, rumor, and mean online behavior.

"Oh, Susan," I say. "Why are you on that website? It's full of hate and intolerance."

Susan sighs.

"I know that now," she says. "There are some girls saying some really mean things about me."

I am shocked to hear this. Susan is the type of person who is so sweet that she'd give chocolate cavities.

"About you? Who would say anything bad about you? You're like the nicest person in the world."

"Here," Susan says. She clicks on a couple of links and sure enough there are conversation threads that specifically make fun of Susan, calling her ugly and making fun of her ethnic background. Other kids have joined in, as kids can do, piling on and calling her other sorts of names as well. Names too insulting to repeat.

I bite my lip as I study the screen trying to determine the date stamps that would let me know how long this activity has been going on. For confirmation, I say, "How long has this been going on?"

"The past two weeks. Since I beat that girl Wendy Parker from Thomas Jefferson in the regional academic triathlon."

Jealousy is a main reason kids bully one another. There are other reasons too, but jealousy is truly a big green-headed monster.

"Wendy Parker started this?" I ask. I don't know Wendy Parker, but her name has been associated with lots of troubling incidents that involved other students to include hazing, and on one occasion, fighting.

Susan nods. She clicks on the first conversation thread that starts this escalation in insulting, name-calling. I see the hurtful comments and immediately feel bad for what I've read. I can only imagine how painful it must feel for Susan.

"I don't want to go to school now," Susan says. "Some of the kids have read these boards and are calling me the same names."

"That's not right," I say. "But you shouldn't give into it. That's what they want you to do. They want to know that their hurtful words have an effect."

"That's easy for you to say," Susan says. "It's not happening to you."

"You're right," I reply. "But that doesn't mean we can't put an end to this. You are not any of the things they say you are. You know that. Your friends know that. Your family knows that. You have value and we all recognize it."

Susan sighs. She struggles to fight back the tears that are threatening to come.

"You know," she says. "Being bullied over the Internet is worse. It's torment and hurts ways that a punch or hair-pulling don't even come close. They say, sticks and stones may break my bones, but words will never hurt me. But you know what? That quote is a lie. Sticks and stones may cause nasty cuts and scars, but those cuts and scars will heal. Insults hurt and sometimes take forever to heal."

I put my arm around and give her a hug.

"You can't tell anyone about this, okay? Promise?"

"We'll figure something out, Susan. That I do promise."

After spending some time with Susan and leaving her in a better mood, I walk back to my father's car. Cyber bullying is rampant among kids who use the Internet to spread their hate and to harass their victims.

My father puts down the book he's reading.

"I thought I was going to have to call in a rescue squad to find you," he jokes, - trying to lighten whatever is weighing heavy on my mind just then. "Everything okay?"

I just sit there, biting down on my lower lip. I can tell my father's looking at me, waiting me to work through my thought process before saying anything else. After a few more moments of weighing the question I'm going to ask him, I turn to my dad.

"Dad," I say. "I have a problem."

"Well, you know I'm always here to help you if you need it," he says. "What can I do?"

I pause before speaking. I don't take lightly telling my parents the names of my friends that are in trouble unless it's very necessary. In this case, I do believe he needs to know.

"Susan is being bullied," I say.

My father nods his head.

"That's something for the school and her parents to address," he says.

"No," I correct myself. "She's being cyber bullied."

My father's face registers the change of information. Again, he nods, as he thinks.

"Cyber bullying is a serious problem," he says. "Remember the cyber conference I went to last month? They had a panel on cyber bullying and how it's becoming more and more prevalent in schools. Not just high school, but middle school, as well. I learned that nearly half of all adolescents in the United States have been bullied online, and equally as many have bullied other people themselves.

"Wow," I say. "That's a lot of people."

"There's more. Did you know the lasting effects of cyber bullying can have fatal consequences? Some teens resort to suicide in a last desperate attempt to escape the trauma caused by this type of bullying."

"That's horrible. I don't want this happening to Susan."

"Neither do I."

My father reaches out to me and brings me close to him and kisses my head.

"Thank you for coming to me with this, Willy," he says. "It takes a lot of courage. I know the premium you place on protecting your friends, and you don't always want to let us know who it is. But this is exactly when it's right to let adults know what is happening so any problems can be immediately fixed. Don't worry. I'll call the Tanakas when we get home."

The next day is Saturday and my father meets me downstairs with a breakfast sandwich.

"Breakfast on the go," he says.

"And where are my two cyber sleuths headed today?" my mother asks, as she pours herself a cup of coffee.

"The Tanakas," my father answers. He turns to me. "Thanks to Willy, here, there is a cyber problem that requires both of our help. I talked to Mr. Tanaka last night and he would like to see us to discuss the next steps."

"That's great," I say.

"Should I be worried?" my mother asks. She always approaches things from the worried parent perspective.

"Not at all," my father says. "We are going to nip this in the bud."

At the Tanaka house, we sit with Susan and her parents.

"This is horrible," Mr. Tanaka says. "How can children be so cruel?"

"If you think about it, Hiroshi," my father says. "It's always been that way. Only now they can do it 24 hours a day because of the Internet."

"He's right," Mrs. Tanaka says. "When we were their age, kids bullied younger and weaker kids. I was bullied by the popular girl clique in high school until they moved onto other girls."

A heavy sigh from Mr. Tanaka.

"I understand," he says. "I guess the more important question is, what we can do now?"

"The first thing is to make sure Susan doesn't respond or reply to any of the online taunting," my dad says. "Responding back will only fuel the fire. Bullies look for that reaction so that they continue the harassment."

"I didn't respond once," Susan says. Honest."

"Good for you," I say. I'm proud of Susan. Not many kids have the strength not to strike back when provoked.

"I believe you, Susan. I'm happy to hear that. Instead of perpetuating the hostile exchanges, you should keep evidence of their bullying. Record dates, times, and descriptions of incidents whether they occur in text messages, emails, or online boards like this one."

"I can teach you how to keep screen shots," I tell my friend.

"Then you do what I call the *three reports*. Report the bullying to the online service providers, report it to the school, and report it to law enforcement," my dad says.

"That's smart, Dad," I say. "Cyber bullying should violate the terms of service that most social media sites and ISPs have."

"That's right, Willy."

"Is law enforcement really necessary?" asks Mr. Tanaka. "It seems like they have other more important things to worry about than kids being impolite."

"That's a good question," my dad says. "Kids will be kids, and name-calling or insult exchanges doesn't necessarily raise to the level of cyber bullying. However, when messages involve threats of violence, sending sexually explicit messages or photos, or escalates into stalking, then believe me, a crime has been committed and the police need to be informed. A quick review of a state's laws will tell you more, and you can always just ask local law enforcement for guidance."

"Since cyber bullying can cause a disruptive element in school, notifying administrators can help them identify the problem, and develop strategies to counter and reduce bullying," I say.

"Wow," Susan chimes in. "I didn't realize there were so many things I could do."

"Don't feel bad, Susan. Many people don't. That's why it's always good to ask someone. Educating yourself is the first step in protecting yourself. Young people are not the only ones who get cyber bullied, you know. And just for the record, adults can be victims too," my father says.

"Thank you, Mr. Paige, for your help," says Mrs. Tanaka.

"Don't thank me. Thank your daughter for reaching out to her friend." He pats me on the back.

I blush and smile and glance over at Susan who already looks like the weight of the world has been lifted from her shoulders.

"Want to get some ice cream?" I ask.

"Double chocolate for me!" Susan shrieked.

My father looks over at Mr. Tanaka.

"How about you guys? I'm buying," my father says.

"Oh, no," says Mrs. Tanaka. "This is our treat."

"I come from good stock."

Chapter Ten

"Isn't that Josie?" my father asks as we turn down our street. I look out the window and see Josie sitting on our front steps. My mom must be at the hospital or else she would have let my friend inside and probably given her some cookies and milk.

"I hope she's okay," I say.

My father parks in our driveway. We get out of the car.

"Hello, Josie," my father says.

"Hello, Mr. Paige. I hope you don't mind me waiting out here."

"Not at all," he says. He gets out his keys and opens the front door. "I take it you're here to see, Willy. I'll let you girls be. You all need something, come inside or give me a holler."

He goes inside the house and I turn to my friend.

"How are you feeling?" I ask her.

She smiles and nods her head.

"Good," she says. "Much better. My parents are not pressing charges against Stevie or his parents. Apparently, when his father found out, he went ballistic. He grounded him for six months and is making him do community service. They came over the other night and he had Stevie apologize to me. He was crying by the end of it."

"I'm glad to hear that," I say. "How have your parents been?"

"They've been really great. They've been very supportive, and they have involved me in everything that's been going on. Here I thought they were going to disown me or send me to a convent or something. But we sat down together and talked through everything and they never raised their voice once. They even set me up with a counselor, so I could discuss the events that led up to me sending him those types of pictures. She's really nice."

"I'm so happy for you," I say. This is a huge relief for me. There can be so much mental and emotional damage for victims of sexting.

"I owe you," she says.

"Are you crazy? We're friends."

"But your business," she says. "A favor for a favor, right? Well, I wanted to let you know that I'm going to pay it forward. I talked to Principal Miller and she is going to let me give a talk about the dangers of sexting at a class assembly."

"That's great! I'm so proud of you, Josie!"

"I know it's only one favor, but…"

I interrupt my friend.

"But nothing," I tell her. "It's perfect."

And with that I put my arm around my friend's shoulder and lead her inside my house.

"Let's share the news with my dad."

Before bed, I sit at my desk and take out my notebook and write down Josie's name. Once empty, my notebook is now full of names of people that I've helped, and now will be helping other people. I feel a strong satisfaction in looking at the names representing people from different backgrounds, different nationalities, different economic levels.

The one thin line connecting all of them is computers. The Internet is a great resource with an abundance of information that's accessible by a simple click of the mouse or touch of your fingertip.

But as powerful a medium as it is, dangers lurk behind every email, application, every IM. That's the problem with the Internet. There is so much bad stuff that can happen to you or your computer if you don't understand the threats that exist, and more importantly, don't understand how to keep yourself safe in cyberspace.

A knock at the door gets my attention.

"Come in," I say.

My father walks inside. He's smiling and holds something behind his back that I can't quite see.

"So," he says to me. "Did the Oracle have a good day?"

"Yes," I say. "Actually, the past two months have been good. I was a bit worried if I would be able to really help people. What I realized is that most people need help when it comes to computer security. Even people like you that work in the field."

"Exactly," he says. "The sooner that everyone realizes that computer security is an ongoing process that is never going away, the sooner things will start to get better. Everything is connected, which means everyone must be involved in making the cyber world a better place. I think it will get there, but it's going to take time."

"Are you going to show me what's behind your back?"

"Ah," he says. "This is for you."

He holds up a thick leather-bound journal.

"What's this for?"

"You've done an impressive job helping those who don't know how to help themselves. It's been a journey of sorts. Not just in the external and digital world, but internally, as well. You've learned things along the way about friends, strangers, adults, and perhaps most importantly, yourself."

"That's true."

He walks over and takes the notebook off my desk.

"You can record your experiences in a cheap notebook," he says. "But your chronicles deserve to be preserved in leather."

He hands me the leather journal. On the cover emblazoned in gold inlay is the following title:

THE WEB PAIGE CHRONICLES.

And now, I'm sharing them with you.

ACKNOWLEDGEMENTS

A great debt of gratitude is owed to Elizabeth Fortin-Hinds who has been extremely helpful in guiding me through the book publishing process, and to Tell-Tale Publishing for taking a chance on this writer.

MORE TIPS FOR IMPROVING PASSWORD SECURITY

- Don't reuse passwords for multiple accounts. A unique password will better ensure that if one has been broken by the bad guys, that all of your online accounts aren't exposed.
- Frequently change passwords is a good practice that will reduce the possibility of potential exposure to hackers.
- Incorporate password phrases of at least eight characters that use upper and lower-case letters, numbers, and special characters.
- Do not share your password with anyone.
- Do not store your passwords on your home computer. If a bad guy breaks into your computer, he will have access to them. Keep passwords in a secure location and not near the computer, such as in an envelope in a bureau drawer.

MORE TIPS FOR SAFEGUARDING INFORMATION ON A COMPUTER

- Password protect important files on your computer and make sure you don't store passwords on the computer to keep them safe.
- Regularly back up any information stored on a computer in the event of an emergency. Malware

isn't the only thing that can make a computer not work or lose valuable files.

- Watch out for suspicious emails. Bad guys prey on users' gullibility to commit their crimes. Do not click on any links or attachments from unknown senders. If a friend or relative does send you something, call them and confirm that they sent you something. The bad guys can make emails look legitimate when in fact they are not.

MORE TIPS FOR SECURING A HOME WI-FI NETWORK

- Turn off your network during extended periods of non-use.
- When installing a wireless home network, the location and physical orientation of the access point or router determines its reach. Position these devices near the center of the home rather than near windows to minimize leakage.
- Turn off Dynamic Host Configuration Protocol on the router or access point, set a fixed private IP address range instead, then configure each connected device with an address within that range.

MORE TIPS TO KNOW IF YOU HAVE SPYWARE ON YOUR COMPUTER

- You are subjected to an endless stream of pop-ups.
- You are redirected to other sites than the one you have typed into your Internet browser.
- Your Internet browser's homepage has hanged.
- Your computer suddenly seems very slow when opening programs or processing tasks such as saving files.
- Unexpected tool bars appear in your web browser.

MORE TIPS FOR POSTING ON SOCIAL MEDIA

- Do not share personal identifiable information such as your birth date, home address, telephone number, or information that can be used by criminals to commit identity theft.
- Do not post pictures that geotag your location as your location will be included in the picture's metadata.
- Do not post anything potentially embarrassing that you wouldn't want your employer or family to know.
- Do not share any information about another person without getting their permission.

MORE TIPS REGARDING DOWNLOADING MOBILE APPS

- It's always good to know more about the app other than the game itself. A little Internet research into the developer of the game, as well as any reviews, comments, or complaints can provide some early indication if the game or the developers behind it are credible and safe.
- Less permissions enabled. Sometimes when you install an app that there are certain permissions that appear. Sometimes they are necessary for the app to function, and other times they are not (for example, access to user information, call history, Internet). Always ensure that permissions are appropriate with the app's functionality is supposed to do
- Make sure your smartphone has security software to scan every app you download. Just like any antivirus program, this will scan the app for any known malware.
- Backup your data. In case a nasty string of malware forces you to wipe your phone clean and start over, a backup of important data will save

MORE TIPS TO PREVENT SEXTING

- Think about the consequences before taking or sending such pictures. An illegal act, the consequences of underage sexting can have severe negative impacts against a person's reputation, the way they are perceived by friends and family, and most important of all, to the individual emotional wellbeing.

- Never take an image of yourself that you wouldn't want your friends, classmates, teachers, and family to see. Once sent, you can't control where the photo goes or who sees it.
- Report any sexting photographs you receive on your phone to an adult that you trust. The sooner the right people are involved, the sooner the situation can be resolved without causing embarrassment to you or the person in the photo or having to suffer legal repercussions for transmitting illegal underage photos.

MORE TIPS FOR STAYING SAFE FROM PREDATORS

- Never download images or click on links from someone you don't know. These can contain inappropriate content and/or malware to infect your computer system.
- Never reveal personal information online to anyone. This includes information about family, friends, school, home address, phone number, email address.
- Choose gender neutral screen names/chat names. This is to ensure that you can't be identified by age, sex, or any other personal information that can identify you.

- Never agree to meet someone you met on-line.
- Be wary of what people say as it may not necessarily be the truth.

MORE TIPS TO PROTECT YOURSELF FROM CYBER BULLYING

- Don't blame yourself – it's not your fault.
- Don't be an accomplice and forward any hurtful messages to other kids.
- Tell a trusted adult about the problem. If a parent is not available find another adult to confide in like a family relative, family friend, or a teacher.
- Never post personal information or private details for the public to see.
- Block communication from the bully.

ADDITIONAL ONLINE RESOURCES

Best Parental Control Software
http://www.pcmag.com/article2/0,2817,2346997,00.asp
ConnectSafely.org
http://www.connectsafely.org/tips-to-help-stop-cyberbullying/
Enhancing Child Safety & Online Technologies
http://cyber.law.harvard.edu/pubrelease/isttf/
Federal Trade Commission/Protecting Kids Online
https://www.consumer.ftc.gov/topics/protecting-kids-online
HelpGuide.org
http://www.helpguide.org/articles/abuse/cyberbullying.htm
Safekids.com
http://www.safekids.com/
StopBullying.gov
https://www.stopbullying.gov/index.html

About the Author

Emilio Iasiello is the author of the short story collection *Why People Do What They Do,* and a nonfiction book, *Chasing the Green.* He has published poetry in several university and literary journals and written the screenplays for several independent feature films and short films and has had stage plays produced in the United States and United Kingdom. A cyber security expert, Emilio has more than 15 years of experience in cyber threat intelligence leading teams in the public and private sectors. He has delivered cyber threat presentations to domestic and international audiences and has published extensively in peer-reviewed journals and cyber security blogs. He lives in Virginia with his wife and two amazing children.

Tell-Tale Publishing would like to thank you for your purchase. If you would like to read other books by this or other fine TT authors, please visit our website:

www.tell-talepublishing.com

CPSIA information can be obtained
at www.ICGtesting.com
Printed in the USA
LVHW08*1034030918
588990LV00006B/23/P